STARSHIP TO DEMETER

STARSHIP PORTALS BOOK ONE

K.D. LOVGREN

GREY KESTREL PRESS

Cover design: Jeff Brown Graphics

Editors: Emmie Mears of Chimera Editing, Keith Morrill of Little City Editing

To be notified of new releases and future books in the Starship Portals series, sign up here: www.kdlovgren.com

For adventurers all

CONTENTS

1

DARK PHASE

THE TRICK WITH THE PORTAL WAS, IT WASN'T ALWAYS VISIBLE. To be more precise, it wasn't always there.

Kal maneuvered the ship in the shadow of Saturn, facing the locus of space where the portal should be.

It needed to be now, or they had wasted months of travel and close to a trillion dollars.

She knew she'd find it. It lurked there, a presence, waiting to be seen. She had been better at getting through the first portal, Freya, than any other pilot. The second portal had never been her mission, luckily, as it turned out. Maybe if she'd been there, it wouldn't have gone wrong. The less said about that disaster, the better.

Her gift for bringing a ship to and through a portal was the real reason she was here, piloting the *Ocean*, years before her time.

This was the furthest mission to inhabit a planet ever conceived.

The crew wouldn't be able to see the swirl of infrared

color, the aura around the portal, until they were so close there was no going back.

"Activate helical search pattern," she said. "Lock on infrared signature."

Because of their proximity to the portal, they were already in dark phase. No transmission possible, to Mars or to home, which made communications quiet. It was easier to concentrate.

"Rai, angle of approach?" Kal said.

"Two degrees short to starboard."

Kal made an adjustment.

The ships' AIs no longer attempted to pilot through the portals, since the starship *Carys*. Feel had something to do with it, and feel was something even a sophisticated iteration like their AI, Rai, didn't have.

Captain Sasha Sarno sat in her chair, center of bridge, strapped in, as all the crew were, for the jump. Seven passengers; seven crew. The passengers were strapped into one of the escape pods with one crew member, just in case. One pod had made it back to Earth when the starship *Carys* disappeared in the second portal.

That job, being the sole crew member strapped in with the passengers, separated from the rest of the team, was not a coveted one. It implied a lack of faith, a lack of commitment, that no crew member wanted to appear to embrace. The volunteer was consequently viewed as heroic.

Noor, mission specialist and analyst, had offered. Kal wished Noor were here on the bridge with Sasha and herself. They had become a triumvirate of sorts, in the months it had taken them to make the loop de loop past Venus, Venus again, then Earth and Jupiter, taking the gravity assist needed off the planets for the best shot to Saturn. After their long winter's nap in hypersleep, post slingshot, it didn't feel like time had passed, despite the months spent under. Even so, they hadn't quite recaptured the banter and ease from before. Maybe after the portal. After the hairiest moment in a trip full of dangers.

The infrared layer was on, covering the whole of the curving window at the front of the bridge. Infrared lit the space around them with strange lights and colors and threw Saturn into brilliant relief, layers of color reflecting the heat signature of each part of the ringed planet, like a slice of an archeological dig into strata of rocks from different eras. The view became magical, touched with fantasy, another way to see space they weren't usually privy to.

Of the three portals discovered, Wóhpe was the most recent. The Aldortok Consortium had sole rights to it so far, and this would be the second jump through.

Thanks to entangled quantum particles on the *Land* and the *Ocean*, they knew they were a go. That was all they knew.

Though little was yet known or understood about the portals, they were believed to have been created millennia before, by an unknown intelligence. One that liked to jump around through systems with habitable planets, and had the advanced knowledge to make it possible. That was the theory.

The seven passengers had been in hypersleep since Earth, unaware of any of the tension of slotting the ship into the mere four hundred kilometer window near Venus to grab the correct trajectory. It was best for them to leave Earth in good shape and have none of the stress, and not get in the way, until it was time to jump the portal on the dark side of Saturn.

In anticipation of the jump, the passengers were now

awake. Everyone would rather be conscious, when it came right down to it, if they were about to blink out in the portal. By unspoken consent, they would all rather know the end, if it was to be so, and not sleep their way into another kind of unknown.

Most of the crew had jumped before, through Freya, as part of the ongoing exploration and establishment of infrastructure on the Earth-like planet in that system.

The second portal, Physis, the one no one liked to mention, hadn't been so trustworthy. The story of what happened to the *Carys* haunted everyone, and no one could be said to approach this jump with anything other than an equal mixture of excitement and dread, except for the captain, Sasha, who didn't get rattled by much of anything.

Kal felt her heart rate bump up. She couldn't see it yet, the spray of light radiating out from a center of deep black, but she could feel it. She could feel they were close, as if the cells in her body shifted their contents toward a source of attraction, a gravity created from inside the portal itself, just ahead, drawing her to it.

The inevitability of it—waiting for her eyes to tell her all choice was over—gave her whole being a charge, as if sparks could shoot from her fingertips, rays from her eyes, waves of heat from her brain, all visible in the same infrared that allowed the portal to be seen.

Their ship, the *Ocean*, the twin of the *Land* already on Demeter with the skeleton crew of biohab builders, was large enough to transport many more passengers. Although on this jump the total count, including passengers and crew, was small, the ships would transport vaster numbers in future, if all went well.

The ships' elegant design, practical and imaginative,

made these two sisters the finest in any fleet, in Kal's opinion, experimental or not.

Kal thought the ships deserved a voyage this far, this uncertain, to prove themselves. She deserved it too. Whether her mettle would be as worthy as the *Ocean*'s remained to be seen.

"Power down inessential systems," Sasha said.

Kal wondered if Sasha could feel the proximity, too.

"Power down inessential systems, confirm," Gunn, systems engineer, repeated.

"Employ stabilization boost, thirty percent. When portal lights become visible, up to seventy-five." Sasha's voice was calm and even. She spoke clearly, with enough volume for all those on the bridge to hear her. In the occupied pod, they had transmission of all that was spoken on the bridge, in case a last minute order to eject was necessary.

Gunn echoed her.

Sasha said, "Pod one: Noor, all set?"

"Aye, Captain." Noor's voice was confident. Strong for the passengers.

As if a veil had been lifted from another reality, the swirl of lights from the portal splayed into view. Radiant, enticing, forbidding: a small gasp from the six on the bridge couldn't be disguised by their cloak of professionalism. It was too beautiful.

No more time to turn back, even had they wanted to. They belonged to the portal, now.

"Stabilization boost, seventy-five percent," Gunn said.

Sasha spoke. "Rai, cede all control to Kal barring mission critical failure or loss of consciousness by Kal and myself. Kal has the helm."

"Yes, Captain. Ceding all control to Kal, barring mission

critical failure or loss of consciousness by Kal and Captain Sarno. Kal has the helm."

This directive had a somewhat dampening effect on the bridge, as Kal was sure it did in the pod. She imagined Noor's wry smile. If Noor were here, they would have exchanged glances.

"Take a breath, everyone," Sasha said, her voice now light. "We made it this far. Keep breathing and we'll celebrate on the other side."

The smile in her voice lifted the lull, and Kal felt herself smile, facing this deepest, darkest, most enchanting circle of blackness, the heart of the portal, and now she felt with her whole being that, yes, she wanted to dive into it, with all of her mind and body. She had never jumped this portal.

Her hands rested lightly on the console, eyes automatically sweeping the mechanical dials, switches, and buttons, a system backup this ship designer always included in case of a shift into low power mode, as well as the latest screened and holographic image processes. Redundancy, a back door in case the front door shut, was such a key part of their survival prospects this far out that the analog was never completely dismissed in favor of the digital or biomorg.

Now Kal was on her own version of autopilot. Her mind was in the trance it went to when she had to be the ship, to navigate it as herself from one difficult spot to another.

"Deploy oxygen," Kal said. They all put their masks on.

"Estimated thirty seconds to entry," Kal said. Her voice was a monotone.

Her heart beat slow. The lights gave the illusion of rushing towards them, reaching out to enfold them, spatters of gold embracing the ship in forgiving splendor, welcoming them to whatever their fate would be.

"Captain?" Gunn said.

The captain was behind Kal, so Kal couldn't see her face.

"It's all right, Gunn," Sasha said.

A brilliant, blinding flash of light.

The light was gone.

The flash an imprint on Kal's retinas.

The only light the remnants in her eyes.

Darkness, incomprehensible.

A compression, emptiness—where time should be.

Kal felt the months in hypersleep stretch inside her.

Her mind hadn't known the passing of time, but something had recorded it.

This place.

Now she knew, the lost time was still there, inside her.

It was here, inside the outside, within the portal.

Here she met time and its absence.

They were lost here, forever.

There was nothing to fly. Her hands were empty.

Smooth and powerless.

A heart-tearing leap, guts on the floor.

The pinpoint, themselves, a universe bursting out of Kal's chest.

A blink, elsewhere, a hand the size of a galaxy.

Light like a resurrection.

Spatter of unfamiliar stars, a planet with rings like Saturn, not Saturn.

They were on the other side.

Had she left those months in the portal?

2

SEXTANT

AFTER THE JUMP, SILENCE.

Kal hoped she hadn't actually left part of her insides in the portal, because it felt that way. Her scooped-out solar plexus made it hard to speak, as well as the curious sensation of having passed through high Gs within, not without. There had been no force driving her back into her seat. It was an internal miscalibration, something essential flipped or removed. She opened her mouth to speak to Rai. No sound came out.

Her mask was still on. She took it off and stared, dazzled by the sights out the window. She heard Sasha's voice.

"Congratulations, everyone. Rai, full systems and hull check. Pod one: You all right?"

Noor's voice came through, "Yes, Captain. Some nausea here. Lost one for a minute there, but he's coming back around. All well."

The crew began to clap, for a brief but enthusiastic smattering of sound, before returning their full attention to their jobs.

System checks and re-check. Rai's rundown and report of impact. Oscillation at some undetermined phase of the jump had thrown off the secondary landing sensors, which required Rai to recalibrate and test them.

The *Ocean* appeared to have sailed through beautifully.

The passengers were loosed from the pod by captain's orders. Ship's doctor Inger and ship's neuropsychologist Chyron left the bridge to give each one a once-over. For the crew's checkups, Inger would wait until things calmed down, here in another part of the galaxy.

As soon as they were through, Gunn started attempting to retrieve information left for them on a mini-satellite supposed to be orbiting whatever planet was nearest. When she gave the sign she had it, another cheer went up.

Noor, now back in her usual place, opened the information in holo form. A three-dimensional map of this part of the system, all the *Land* had been able to glean, displayed before them.

Planetary objects were labeled. The *Land*'s crew had named things. The close ringed planet, a sister of Saturn, Kal thought, was labeled Sextant. The sun, Mythos.

Noor analyzed the coordinates and announced, "We're not that far from the center of the Milky Way."

Kal was transfixed by the new view from the bridge, while noting the ship's velocity vector relative to Sextant, still on her version of autopilot. Sextant had rings like Saturn and a similar majestic presence, but there was no mistaking it for Saturn.

Sextant was much smaller, with tighter rings. Its opalescence was a shock to Kal, as was the far-dappled light of strange constellations. A sprinkle of stars in a curve, with a brighter line behind them, looked like an archer with bow.

Sextant was warmer, less forbidding than Saturn, the pale green and blue swirl eclipsed by a glittery veiled glow of cloud, like the layers of shifting color on an opal ring held to the light. Her rings were wide and airy, a dust storm radiating in ordered plumes around her.

They couldn't see Demeter from where they were, or Mythos, the star at the center of this system. Demeter was the next planet over, but they had emerged on the far side of Sextant. Like the earlier portal, this one was probably fixed to its home planet, Sextant, by some gravitational force scientists back home were still arguing over. The portals in Earth's solar system orbited to remain on the dark side, the side unviewable from the habitable planet it was presumably created to access.

Kal took a deep, shuddering breath that felt like it could crack ribs. She snuck a look over her shoulder at Sasha. Sasha was looking at the holo of their new system but must have felt Kal's eyes on her.

Sasha turned her head. "Good work, Kal." Then she gave a nod with a slow blink, which was even better.

With a sketch of a salute Kal turned back to the controls.

Noor glided in at a brisk pace, her face alight in contrast to her usual scientist's calm. Her mind might be full of calculations and ideas for a future paper, Kal knew, but she registered both the scientific and emotional aspects of a milestone when they achieved one.

Noor briefed the captain in an undertone. When she was done she joined Kal at the console.

"How was that?" Kal asked Noor, her eyes sharing the light in Noor's.

Noor pursed her lips. "You didn't have vomit duty." Her grin broke through.

"You took one for the team, sister," Kal said, one eye on her holo.

Noor swung into a seat next to Kal, not her usual one, but her usual chatting-to-Kal one.

"Who was the worst?" Kal asked, occupied with the holo imaging on the landing system but able to talk at the same time.

"Yarick threw up. He was my old thesis advisor, so that was satisfying. Tafari passed out. They'll both get an extra scan and fluids."

"The rest okay?" Kal asked.

"Terrified, but they hid it well. Troupers. Struggled with the suits a bit."

"That was something, huh?" Kal couldn't believe she'd done it. She'd been the one. Even though it felt like control had shifted at some point, as if she were guiding the ship with her thoughts and not her body, which she didn't quite want to talk about. Whatever had happened, she'd piloted them through.

"You crushed it," Noor said, her voice unemphatic but her rare smile making it special. Her dark eyes were luminous, like Sextant. Her black hair was tied back in a high ponytail, as Kal's was in her usual braid. Everyone's hair had been scraped back for the portal.

"Thanks," Kal said, feeling the quiet satisfaction of her friend's appreciation.

They surveyed the vast planet near them, its wide dusty rings, the infinite space surrounding it, for a long time. Neither had to speak.

And it was dark phase, so they really were free.

Dark phase was the best part of the trip for Kal.

It was quiet, a respite from the busier, nosier times on

each end of an interplanetary journey. People on planets always wanted information. When in dark phase, the information on the ship *Ocean* was self-contained, carried with them. No communications back and forth would be possible until they were out of range of the portal and in range of Demeter. They were replete.

Those times Kal was alone on deck she was captain and adventurer, like the seafarers of old. Even if she was the pilot, not the captain.

"We're going to drill today." Sasha spoke for the benefit of the whole bridge. "Since we didn't have time before the jump, we have to get it done before they sleep again."

None of the passengers had participated in a safety drill yet, since they were fresh out of hypersleep.

Noor stood. "Captain, Inger said the passengers should be through their debrief by sixteen hundred."

"We'll set it for seventeen hundred, then. Noor, you've had less sleep than most of us, prepping the passengers. Why don't you grab a nap before the drill."

Noor usually covered the bridge at night.

"Will do," Noor said. She glanced at Kal in private alarm. Kal knew they were all so adrenalized from the jump it would be a challenge for anybody to sleep in the near future. Kal shrugged.

"I'll go for a quick run, get my head clear," Noor announced.

"See you soon," Kal said.

Sasha unstrapped herself and stood, stretching her arms over her head. "Rai, please announce the drill at seventeen hundred hours. Mandatory."

Sasha's hair reminded Kal of the color of the hickory nuts her aunt used to gather back home. Her even brows and hazel-brown eyes gazed at people with an unconcern that calmed the anxious and rattled the disingenuous.

Rai acknowledged the command and it soon echoed through the ship, the captain's words in Rai's voice.

In the vaulted greenhouse adjoining the park, during a break before the drill, Kal found solace in the dirt. The black and purple iris in her hands fell apart easily at the new rhizome as she shook it and insinuated her thumb in its divide. Just when she was getting in the groove, Kal heard signs of a visitor, footsteps accompanied by the *tap tap* of a cane. As she placed one of the bulbs in the hollow of dirt she had dug, a shadow loomed over her shoulder, cutting off the wavering light from above.

The person proved to be the passenger Yarick. His build was slight but wiry, silvery brown hair brushed smooth from a side part. The grooves between nose and mouth showed him to be older than most of the travelers. There was a tweedy look about him, a professorial air. Noor's little comment about him had Kal's antennae up. Was he merely seeking refuge in the greenery, or looking for someone to talk to? Or to corner?

"Ah, the infamous Kal Black Bear," he said.

Kal stood up, trowel in her hand. "Infamous? You flatter me."

He stepped back a couple of paces, propping his cane and balancing both hands on it. "Quick up through the ranks, talented, daring. It was unexpected for you to pilot such a mission so soon, wouldn't you agree?"

Kal looked over the beds of flowers and herbs, the taller

shrubs and small trees dotted throughout. "Maybe. I don't know if that makes me infamous. Infamous sounds pretty bad." Kal made a villain face and twirled an imaginary mustache.

"Famous then. In certain circles," Yarick said.

With no idea what he was getting at, Kal said nothing. She knew she was a good pilot. She settled on a neutral smile.

"The greenhouse and park are very nice. A respite from all the carbon and titanium," Yarick said, rotating to look.

"Yep." She spun the trowel, trying to remember his CV. Some AI guru with a lot of money and pull.

"You're First Nations."

It seemed he didn't know everything. "That's right. Sort of. I'm not Canadian."

"Of course. Sorry. You were specially selected, though. Many of the Indigenous were chosen for their experience, their cultural memories, their Earth tie—ironic, in that the mission forces us all to leave that mother of ours behind—and I expect Aldortok would be very happy if you decided to stay on Demeter."

Kal tapped the trowel on her thigh, trying to make him out. She remembered him from the prep time before they left Earth, but he'd come in late. "The whole project is Indigenous and I'm a part of of it, if that's what you mean. I won't be staying permanently. My place is on a ship." He wasn't a sponsor, was he? If he was some noggin they were hauling along because he was a titan of industry, surely she would have heard.

"Are you so sure you won't stay?" Yarick said.

"What do you mean?" She cocked her head slightly, eyes widened. Was he recruiting her for something?

"I mean, you might be more valuable to them there. You

could start a whole new life, in a whole new world. A world unblemished by our ugly Terran history. You could make a difference there. Be a founding mother."

She blinked. "Founding mothers and fathers aren't the best example for me."

"Unless you left someone behind," Yarick continued.

Kal had done interrogations of her own, in another life. His wasn't cutting it.

"Family?" he said. "I have no one, family-wise. No ties that bind. But you. Your DNA must be perpetuated. Have you set an intention of surrogacy?"

She broke out of the reverie of guessing what he wanted. "Uh....that's an interesting question."

"Sorry, sorry." He held his hand up. "If you didn't have any close ties there, you would really be an ideal candidate. I could speak to the board, if you'd like. The captain, now, she also would be a prime candidate for settlement. I despair of appealing to her sense of duty in this matter. She seems bound to her ship. It would seem her destiny would lie here, unless..."

She saw him notice the pricking of her ears at the mention of Sasha. Looking back at the dirt, she tried to appear uninterested, but she wanted to hear what he would say.

He took a step forward, leaning in. "Unless she found someone here, on the ship, decided to start a new life, a new family." His index finger tapped the side of his mouth. "Do you think she's interested in anyone?" He chuckled. "I know there are a few interested in her. We'll keep that between us. The perceptive few can't help but notice."

"Notice what?"

"Notice how everyone falls for the captain. It's charming. Quite a pash they all have for her."

"Like who?" If he was spilling dirt, she wanted to know what was floating around among the passengers.

"If you haven't noticed I wouldn't want to spread gossip," Yarick said, the picture of virtue.

"You mean Gunn, I suppose," Kal said, priming the pump. She felt a little bad for throwing Gunn under the bus.

"Gunn has great loyalty, to be sure. I don't know if it's a grand amour."

Kal traced a line of her palm with the point of the trowel, waiting. When he didn't continue, she said, "You've been awake for less than twenty-four hours. How could you know all this?"

"If you have the eyes to see, much is visible in a short time." He tapped the side of his nose.

Kal made a sound that resembled a snort.

"There's Tafari," he said, seeming to try to keep her interest.

"Tafari." She would just repeat what he said. She didn't think he'd notice.

"Or Haven. Inger?"

"Yourself?" Kal said. She smiled.

He shrugged. "I'm too passive for her. Like I told someone else who asked me, I wouldn't say no."

"I don't think you're her type."

"No. I suppose not. What about you?"

When had Yarick really made all these observations? In the time before he'd been put into hypersleep, on Earth?

The mission's compatibility advisor had used tests more than actual interaction between crew and passengers, before the mission. There hadn't been time, since they had a very limited timespan to launch in order to meet Venus's window. Some of the passengers had been added quite soon before departure. Yarick was one.

"Do you like the captain?" he said.

"Of course I like her. Pretty much everyone does." He'd have to find some better stuff than this if he wanted to uncover crew rumors to go along with his passenger ones.

"You and all the others," he said.

"Quite a number, according to you. You should bring it up with Chyron." The mission neuropsychologist would have a few things to make of his theories, Kal thought.

"Mmm." He looked a little ruffled by that suggestion. "I wonder what Rai thinks. Rai, does Kal have feelings for Captain Sarno? Beyond respect and liking, I mean."

Kal's arm involuntarily twitched. Her mouth opened, but before she could speak, Rai was speaking.

"Privacy concerns prevent me from answering," Rai said.

"Classified, is it? Declassify it."

"Rai," Kal said. "Yarick is not a crew member of this ship."

"Yarick Cole is a former board member of the Aldortok Consortium," Rai said smoothly.

Oh. "Does that give him clearance for private biologic information?" Kal said. "If it does, I'd like to know."

"No, Kal. Unless given permission by Captain Sarno."

"As I thought," Kal said to Yarick, who maintained an irksome smile. Holy hell. This guy could go right out the airlock.

"Captain Sarno might want to know. If I give her a tip." He maintained an expression of bland helpfulness, but she saw the mischief in his eyes. He'd wanted some kind of rise from her and it appeared he'd gotten it.

Yarick laughed and attempted to clap her on the back.

She dropped her shoulder and feinted, so he swished at air, which made him look foolish. She chuckled herself, now. He laughed along, as if the whole exchange was a bonding moment.

"I meant it as a friendly gesture. Apologies. Rai, disregard the following," he said.

"Yes, Yarick," Rai said.

Kal looked up at the roof of the greenhouse, as if she could see Rai.

Yarick read her thoughts. "She can't defy a direct order. We're not overheard now."

"That's not true. There is no such order."

"Captain Sarno gave me a certain latitude, so I could review systems while I'm here. Rai was my baby, once, in an earlier iteration."

"Your baby." Thinking of Rai as an extension or creation of Yarick was unwelcome. Rai was a good sort.

"Yes. She named herself, of course. Her little joke. My greatest achievement, that. An evolution of my creation, a machine who can make a joke, a play on words, the most sophisticated use of language." He seemed to collect himself, patting at his chest pocket and clearing his throat. "I won't say anything to Captain Sarno. I won't ask Rai to prove anything that might be uncomfortable for you. I like you, Kal. You can trust me."

The way his eyebrows came together, crinkling up his forehead, his dewy eyes soft and deer-like now instead of sharp and insinuating, was such a turnabout Kal wanted to laugh again.

The switcheroo from provocative to earnest was so abrupt, along with several other warning bells, that Kal found herself suspicious of everything he said. At the same time her mind winnowed through the implications of all his words, trying to sort the wheat from the chaff.

Yarick seemed to be waiting for a response.

"I will remember everything you said." He wouldn't get much change out of that. And it was true.

Looking pleased with her response, he winked. "It's mostly a joke. Harmless fun. I'll be on my way then."

He turned, deftly for a fellow with a cane, and tapped his way off.

Kal shook her head and threw her trowel down into the bed, where it stuck, point buried in the earth.

She had twenty minutes until the drill.

FOR THE DRILL ITSELF, Kal ran the show. "Are we all here? Where's Noor?"

"Not here yet," Sasha said. "She'll show up. Proceed."

Sif, an Icelandic passenger with a slight lilt to her speech, said, "Yarick isn't here."

Kal looked to Inger.

Inger craned her neck, looking around for Yarick. "He had a rough jump. I'll query his cabin."

Kal thought he'd looked well enough when he'd bothered her.

"It's fair to say we all might feel out-of-sorts the next few days," Kal said to the group. "Not quite yourselves. A jump is enough to scramble your insides and your outsides. Check in with Chyron, or Inger, or any of the crew you feel comfortable talking to if you feel something much beyond the worst jet lag you've ever had. Welcome to space-time lag."

That got a chuckle from the passengers, who looked varyingly nervy, ecstatic, or dazed, depending on the individual.

"As you know, I'm Pilot Kal Black Bear, and for the newly awake, we do these drills once a week without fail, to keep everyone on their toes and able to respond to a call without having to think too much about it. There will be an unscheduled timed drill in the next few days, since we haven't had the whole group available to do one until now, so be ready for that. We don't anticipate any trouble. It's been a pretty smooth flight so far. And we're through the portal."

This elicited a cheer and hand slaps all round.

Kal picked out the faces around her, matching the holo of faces she'd seen previously with the names on the manifest.

The tall, long-limbed man with a blue-black sheen to his skin must be Tafari, the historian and city planner. The one who'd fainted, she noted. He looked a little gray, but stood with his hands in his pockets and a game look on his face.

One woman wore a silken purple headwrap, close-fitted to her head. Her face was wide, with an imperial air. Short and broad of stature, this must be Ogechi, from Ghana, a novelist and N-Go champion, one of the artists and storytellers of the group. She had professed an interest in playing N-Go with Rai while aboard, as some sort of sociological experiment.

As the group continued to exchange quick words of greeting and expressions of relief and jubilation over completing the jump, Kal realized Sif, the woman who had spoken earlier, was standing close to her.

"We both have three letters in our names," Sif said. "We're alike." Her pleasure in this seemed genuine.

With a smile, though Sif was technically interrupting the drill, Kal said, "My full name is Kaliska."

Sif said, "Never mind then," and turned away, snubbing Kal as if Kal deserved it.

Kal's eyes widened and she caught Gunn watching her. Gunn was also an Icelander. Kal didn't know if she and Sif were friends, but Gunn's expression was critical, whether of Kal or Sif, Kal couldn't tell. Kal tried not to be intimidated by Gunn, but it wasn't easy. Gunn could bench press any two of the other travelers here and probably whistle a tune at the same time.

Kal brought her thoughts back to what she was doing. The self-congratulation over the successful jump was winding down, and the group was attentive again.

"Now," Kal said, "will you all please take your places in your assigned pods. You're split into two this time, not all in pod one like the jump. Get back into your exosuits...I know, I know. It's part of the drill. Be warned, next time will be a practice emergency timed drill and at a much faster pace. Get better at it. Last one in will be a rotten egg. You don't want to find out what that means."

The six passengers present split into two of the four pods, three in each. The other two pods were redundancy only.

Kal, Sasha, and Inger stood outside the pods, looking up and down the corridor. Inger shook her head; no answer from Yarick's cabin.

"Rai," Sasha said, "Locate Mission Specialist Noor Sultana and passenger Yarick Cole. Tell them the drill is waiting."

"Yes, Captain."

3

DYADS

NOOR TRIED TO SLEEP, BUT IT DIDN'T COME. KNOWING SHE HAD to wake for the drill soon didn't help. Resigned, she took a shower and set off to check on some of her experiments while she waited for the excitement of the portal to wind down. It could take time to get over the space-time lag, in any case.

There would be time enough to check her experiments in zero G and get to the drill on time.

When Noor entered cargo airlock seven, she traveled between the atmospheric gravity of the ship and the zero gravity of space.

The procedure between doors was tedious. When Noor was in the airlock, she had to wear one of the light suits. Thinner, more comfortable, and maneuverable than the exosuits, they were nonetheless difficult to put on. They fit closely over the skin, requiring her to strip down to her skivvies to don one. A small pile of Noor's clothes could be found outside the hatch when she was inside.

While she was in the airlock she floated in zero G, her oxygen supplied by the suit, which had a self-contained helmet like the larger suits, with a second visor that could be raised or lowered, depending on whether someone was in zero G or not, exposed to bright light or not.

The lack of atmosphere was a vacuum. If a suit were compromised, exposure to the vacuum was not a disaster, as long as the person got back to oxygen or atmosphere soon enough. It wasn't a desirable experience, but accidents happened on occasion.

Noor divested herself of her clothes, wriggled into the light suit, attached her helmet, released the hatch door, slithered through the stretchy skin that divided the hatch and the airlock, sealed the hatch door, and depressurized the airlock, to get it back to a vacuum.

Once the vacuum was re-established, she opened the experiment chamber and went about her usual routine of checking the instruments and data. It was nauseating to flip from pulling regular Gs to the zero G space. She always had to fight the urge to vomit. Once the worst of that passed, she sometimes floated around for a while, looking out the window in the cargo door, doing somersaults, and throwing some 360 yoga moves such as she could usually only do in the physio.

After the experiment check, she was trying a 180, flipping one way, then the opposite, since there was no 'up' in the vacuum, when she felt a difference in her oxygen level. It could only be a leak. Her oxygen was streaming out somewhere below her visor, where it was usually sealed tight. She flipped down the sun visor, the second layer that was used for welding work or when exposed to bright light, to see if it would click and seal. It didn't. She tried to feel the spot where it was leaking, to block the stream. She got her finger on it. There must be another leak, because the air quality continued to deteriorate.

"Rai, alert, helmet failure. Oxygen deficit."

There was no answer. Unless she was unable to hear Rai because of the lack of oxygen around her ears. She had felt them pop.

With a push of her feet Noor launched herself off the cargo door, across the airlock, toward the hatch. She was close enough to oxygen. A crackling in her ears was the only sound, an interior body sound within, in the wide absence of sound around her. She tried not to gulp the last of her oxygen, but the instinct was so strong she couldn't stop a big breath, which started full and rich and ended flat. She breathed out, the carbon dioxide puffing out into nothing, the last of the air in the balloon. A fizzy bubbling sensation on her tongue told her she was in trouble, the last of the moisture in her mouth evaporating. She had about two to three minutes to get out.

The means to open the hatch was a flat lever the size of a hand to be turned from horizontal to vertical. Once the lever was turned, she would push a large button to release the door and slide through the skin-like membrane. Her muscles still worked. She flipped the lever, breathing in relief, but there was no air to breathe. Her lungs made the movements and got nothing for it. She pressed the button. Nothing happened.

She couldn't stop herself from hammering on the door, though the sound wouldn't carry.

"Rai. Rai." She didn't have air to form words. The red of worry, the deep dark red of danger and rescue, floated in front of her eyes. She pushed her hand at it. Her body was lifted by the vacuum, away from the inner hatch. With a flailing motion of her arms and legs, she reached for the hatch door, but the hull-side cargo door was too far away to push against with her feet and she floated back toward the hull, as if she'd paddled backwards in the ocean.

"Rai." She formed the last word with her mouth.

YARICK COLE, on his new daily perambulation dictated by Inger, saw a small puddle of clothes at the end of the long hall to the hatch. He was exploring, walking every arm and corner of the ship, at his own slow pace. It was better than the physio, to his mind, which resembled nothing so much as a torture device.

He looked at the clothes, then up at the porthole window in the hatch door. Something was floating in there. He crept closer and looked through.

The sight that met his eyes, a body floating, hair seeping out in tendrils from the visor, caused him to slam the emergency open switch, without thinking too clearly about the consequence. The skin of the tube blew back into the hatch, he was sucked toward it, and the floating figure slid away toward the cargo door. Yarick tore at the skin with scrabbling hands, hacking at it with his stick in one hand while he tried to rend it with the other. It didn't want to tear. He launched himself forward into the vacuum, one foot hooked for safety on the stretchy skin.

The stick helped him grab her, the hook on the end encircling her arm. He vomited, the sick floating out in a spray of tiny globules he ignored as he reeled her toward him. With a yank he got her into the tunnel of silky stretchy intermediacy, the portal between death and life.

They were forced out with his desperate pull, like

mammals falling from the womb of a tall creature, splat on the hard ground. Her leg was caught in the skin. On his hands and knees he untangled her and struck at the switch with his cane. It enclosed itself like a mollusk snapping shut as he yanked an oxygen cube from the wall, piercing and pressing it over her mouth.

"Send help." His words wheezed out. "Emergency, send help."

SASHA TOOK over in pod one, Kal in pod two, as they waited to hear back from Rai. Kal studied her passenger manifest as the two passengers in her pod struggled into their exosuits while the crew slipped into theirs like the second skins they had become. Kal used little memory tricks to help her remember the background of the passengers, the better to manage them.

Crew in her pod were Gunn, Inger, and Haven. Big engineer and fix-it person Gunn, MD Inger—a decent sort but testy—and payload specialist Haven, who could crawl through all the cargo holds and not get lost.

Passengers were the missing Yarick (thrower-upper, AI wiz and polymath, former advisor to Noor who Noor appeared to have an antipathy for, nosy parker), Wei (artist, short dark hair swept back in a pompadour, compact and athletic-looking, daughter of somebody famous, Kal couldn't remember who), and Davena (hydroenergy and botany specialist, Maori, rumored not to suffer fools, round and powerful with a bellowing laugh). Pretty good so far.

Davena and Wei were not too bad with the suits. Kal could whip them into shape. It would have been nice to have

Noor in her pod instead of Gunn. She hoped she wouldn't ever have to occupy a pod longterm with Gunn. Better not to let her thoughts go there.

Gunn was strapping in docilely enough at the moment. Red-haired Haven was inward and quiet, as usual. She wasn't very verbal unless necessity required. Haven liked making complex line art with a ruler. And puns. That was Kal's in with Haven.

Everyone else was suited up in pod two and were now strapping in. They were in the oval transport module, the seats ringing the oval so they all faced each other when in place. The crew's seats could be swiveled and slid to other parts of the module depending on what sort of operation was needed. Kal locked her seat facing the oval for this simulation.

The pods' other attached modules, including hypersleep chambers, sleep bay, infirmary, mess, and hydroponic garden, made the pods much larger than they seemed from this compact module where they conducted drills. The pods were fully sufficient for long distance travel, but a far cry from the comfort of the ship.

"Report, pod two." Sasha's voice came over the comm from pod one.

"Suited and strapped in," Kal replied. "No sign of Yarick, Captain."

Before Sasha could respond, a distress call came over the all comm. It was Yarick.

"Rai?" Kal called as she unbuckled as fast as she could.

"Malfunction in cargo airlock seven," Rai said.

Kal hadn't given the order to seal the doors yet and she was up and out of the pod before anyone else had time to react. Lumbering like a bear in the exosuit, she heard Sasha's feet beating behind her.

That airlock was one level up. They stumped up the spiral ramp to the floor above and down the too-long corridor to the dark recesses of airlock seven, their movement lighting up the passage as they went. Down another offshoot arm of the corridor and Kal could see Noor on the floor, Yarick kneeling beside her. He held an oxygen cube to her mouth. Her hair spread around her head, black tendrils, Medusa's snakes transformed into silk.

Kal knelt on the other side of Noor, breathing hard. Running in the exosuit was like running through sand in one point two times the gravity.

Noor was wearing the light suit. If she had been in an exosuit it would have shocked her heart if her heart went out of rhythm or stopped. The light suit couldn't. Closing her fingers around Noor's wrist, Kal felt for a pulse while she leaned down, pushing Yarick and the cube out of the way to feel for Noor's breath on her cheek.

She couldn't tell if it was the oxygen from the cube rushing out or Noor's breath. Then Inger was there, beside her, moving Kal firmly aside. Inger had retrieved a kit from the wall next to the airlock and set it next to Noor. Kal opened the kit while Inger unzipped Noor's suit. Inger smoothed sensors on Noor's chest, plugged them into the kit, and placed a mask over her face.

Inger waited calmly while the sensors acted. They lit up red and Inger said, "Stay back." They inched away. Noor's body convulsed. The sensor glowed green.

"Sinus rhythm," Inger said. Everyone else was coming forward now, crowding the corridor.

"Get the hell back," Inger barked.

Sasha came forward as Yarick retreated. Sasha squeezed Yarick's arm. "Are you okay?"

He nodded and turned into the cluster of people now in the larger corridor. Chyron supported his arm as he found a place next to her. A space widened around them, the other travelers giving them room.

Inger punched another button beside the airlock and released the bodyboard. She set it next to Noor, then peeled off and placed five magnets on Noor, one on each limb and one on the back of her head.

"No hover transfer. Lift her."

Kal on one side, Sasha the other, with Inger at Noor's head, they moved her on three. The magnets snapped into place and Inger activated the neck brace, which wrapped itself around Noor's neck. Inger set the hover to waist level and they moved with her on the bodyboard, parting the other travelers as they moved through, down the long corridor on the way to the infirmary.

AFTER THE RESCUE—INGER at Noor's side, Yarick's face a study in shock, Noor's transportation to the infirmary and placement in an induced coma—the initial panic was over. In Sasha's mind it was a blur, since Inger had determined all that was to be done. The horror of it was setting in. Everyone except Inger and Sasha had finally gone to bed. Sasha was numb.

She stood on the bridge, haunting Noor's usual spot where Noor worked through the night.

She couldn't go to bed with Noor in a coma, anyway.

They were locked in orbit around Sextant, their first

swing around the planet before they swooped again and caught the gravity assist to Demeter.

Inger wouldn't make predictions.

Sasha's hand brushed the space over the trajector and brought the three-dimensional plot of their path into view. This system, dubbed mythian for its star, Mythos, as their own was called the solar system for the Sun, or *Sol*, had a collection of fourteen planetary bodies in orbit. They were approaching from deeper space, traveling in toward the star Mythos at its center, to reach their planet of choice, the fifth closest to Mythos. Since they had passed the cusp of the sixth planet and entered orbit around it, theoretically the next tricky bit wouldn't come until tomorrow.

Sasha stared at the slowly rotating projection, seeing where they'd come from and where they were going as a faint line of light, navigating through the worlds. She stared for a long time.

They were on a new course, re-calculated by Rai since the portal jump, which brought them closer to Sextant than the original trajectory of the earlier mission. It was a gamble, as Sextant was ringed with planetary asteroid bands like Saturn, giving the ship a moderate danger of interference. Rai calculated and set the odds as minuscule, as long as they stayed at their current velocity vector relative to Sextant before the slingshot, midpoint reversal, and slowdown as they approached Demeter.

Using an image near her, Sasha entered some variables, throwing alternates at the projection to see what-if scenarios play out. Mythian flare, asteroid sheer, and so on. The small slice of mythian system before her rippled in altered states as she forced it through shifts in potential realities. It was soothing. If this, then that. Safe, safe, safe. The ship kept them safe.

Sasha wondered how soon her role might be redundant. Would it ever? Would human cargo always need a human attendant, a monitor to shepherd them through the perils of space? Sasha liked to think yes, for her generation at least. She wondered what Rai would think of this.

Sasha said to the holo, "Ice and asteroid storm promoted by mythian flare, ship adjacent. Forty degrees to starboard relative to Sextant. Planned trajectory." The image rippled. It showed a larger-than-scale model of the ship in the place she had indicated. Specks showered the ship in waves.

Gliding her fingers on the console, Sasha studied the projection. This trajectory still gave her pause. She would ask Rai to perform more analysis in creative mode. Passenger Gwendy Lewis was available, too, for consultation, a back-up trajectorist on contract, who was disembarking longterm on Demeter.

Sasha couldn't talk to Noor about it now.

Later, unsure how much time had gone by, she heard the door of the bridge open and saw Kal.

"Couldn't sleep?" Sasha asked.

"Nope." Kal's eyes were bleary. "Heard anything?"

Sasha shook her head. "Inger said the coma will help her recover faster, like you said. No news other than that."

Kal slumped down in her usual seat. She said, "Have you gone over what happened?"

"I haven't been able to bring myself to watch the holo yet. I need to," Sasha said.

"I'll watch it with you, if you want."

"Thanks, Kal," Sasha said quietly. "Dim lights," she said to Rai. "Bring up cargo seven airlock during Noor's experiment check."

With the room dimmed to grayness, the holo appeared

before them brighter than it would have otherwise. Sasha sat in the seat opposite Kal, the holo between them.

In the holo image, they saw Noor wriggling into the airlock. She sealed the door, re-established the vacuum, and went about her experiments. Watching her floating there was mesmerizing. In the quiet of the night-time ship it was as if they were watching a window opened into the past, which they were. When Noor started doing her stunts in the zero G, Kal and Sasha couldn't help but smile. In this moment it hadn't happened yet. Sasha wished she could freeze Noor there in time.

The next few minutes grew tense, then harrowing. Seeing Noor struggle for air, try to stop the leaks, call through her comm for Rai, struggle to get out through the hatch and fail, was excruciating. It was when Noor's face was flipped up toward the camera and they could read her lips when she had run out of oxygen, what she was saying, still trying to say, that Sasha and Kal's eyes met over the holo with the impact of what had happened. "Rai," she was saying. "Rai."

Rai had not answered. Rai had not helped.

4

RAI

THE TUBE WAS ONE OF THE ONLY SPACES ON THE SHIP NOT IN view of cameras or sensors. It was not literally tube-shaped but had been christened that by a Londoner, one of the ship designers, who thought it had a subway-like feel. It was a couple of rooms, rectangular and lined in a row like a traincar, designed with a nautical air and simplicity, which could be used for private conversations or assignations, as required.

The teak accents of wood and sleek, Art Deco details in the walls and furniture gave the impression of being inside a twentieth-century pre-war yacht rather than confined to an internal chamber without windows, only mock portholes with images to imply they were at sea.

Although consideration for the crew had been a minor concern, it being more designed for the high-profile passenger who might need to have an ears-only conversation, it was utilized by crew and passengers alike, if necessary. No one had made use of it so far on this mission, as far as anyone knew. It was as if no one wanted to be seen to want extra privacy.

No record within.

SASHA AND KAL'S eyes were locked. Noor floated in front of them in the holo, now unconscious, as they waited what seemed an eternity for Yarick to break through.

The image pulsed, like a power surge, Noor's back arching in a spasm while she floated, unaware. The image flickered out. Sasha snapped at Rai to reestablish playback.

Rai informed them a power surge had interrupted transmission. There was nothing more.

Not seeing her rescued was terrible. That last image of her floating, convulsing, trapped forever in a vacuum, could not be erased.

Rai. What Rai had done. What Rai hadn't done. Right there in front of them, in the record.

KAL COULD SEE the slow expansion of Sasha's irises. The muscles from her jaw to her neck were tight.

Fast and slow, instantaneous yet endless, in that moment they had to read each other's minds. How could either of them say anything? Noor had asked for help and Rai had not answered. Rai was going to let Noor die. Noor's comm had worked. Rai had heard her. She had done nothing.

Being alone here on the bridge, the two of them, the rest of the ship asleep except for Inger, far away in the infirmary, Kal felt a dread and fear she'd never known since the first time she'd set foot on a ship. Ships were her home. This ship was her home.

The *Ocean* was life. Rai was life, to them.

After an eternity, stiff like she'd been fished out of ice water, Kal stood up. She didn't know what to do, but she couldn't sit anymore.

Sasha didn't move.

After a longer silence, Kal spoke to Sasha. "I think I'll turn in." They had to get out of here. They couldn't say anything about it. For at least a few breaths, Kal was desperate to leave the bridge, where it felt like Rai's presence was magnified, inescapable.

Sasha reached out and grabbed Kal's wrist. An electric flash burned through Kal. Sasha had never touched her, except to help her in an exosuit.

"Kal," Sasha said. She let her grip on Kal relax. Her fingers followed the trace of Kal's wrist down to her hand, which she wove her fingers into. Kal saw Sasha lick her lips. Kal swallowed.

What was happening? The lights were still dim, with no light from the holo anymore. Was this real? Kal kept those dreams so locked down she didn't let herself think them often, but sometimes, sometimes she did. Had she blacked out in shock? She might open her eyes in the infirmary, with Inger bending over her, any second. Kal blinked rapidly.

"Kaliska," Sasha said. She stood. Her voice was lower than usual, rougher. Her fingertips curved in a rake that carved against Kal's palm. Kal's hand jerked, flat and rigid. She didn't pull away. She couldn't move.

"It's okay." Sasha stood, scanning Kal's eyes, back and forth, back and forth, reading her. "Don't worry. We're in dark phase."

Kal's cheek twitched, under her eye, as if Sasha had

burned her with a laser. Sasha slid her hand up Kal's arm until she held her behind the elbow.

"Come with me to the Tube?" Sasha said.

Sasha's eyes were so intent, unyielding. Kal didn't know what to do. Her career flashed before her eyes, her stripes.

"It will be all right," Sasha said.

"I didn't think, I didn't know...," Kal trailed off.

"It's been a stressful trip. Do you want to kiss me?"

The flickering in Kal blazed out into something stronger, something that wanted to be unleashed. The horror of what had happened to Noor, what might be happening with Rai, made it more real, a call that could be answered.

"Yes."

"Kiss me," Sasha said.

Kal took a step forward, into Sasha's embrace. Sasha's arms slid behind Kal's back. Kal put one hand on Sasha's neck, felt the soft skin under her hair, the thick soft hair where it was gathered at the back of her head. Sasha's expression was blank, unreadable, but her lips parted and Kal kissed her.

Sasha's mouth, the lips Kal had studied so often when Sasha was speaking, the mouth she'd never thought would be hers, felt like coming home. Kal licked her lower lip and slid her tongue in, just a touch. Then they were spinning around, mouths locked, hands in each other's hair, twisting in the air like they were dancing until their bodies met the curve of the wall. Sasha was against it, the subtle flicker of Rai's sensors behind her. Kal took both hands and traced the hair at the sides of Sasha's face, brushing it back, making the shape of a heart with her fingertips, from the center of her part out to her ears and down the line of her jaw. Sasha's head was pressed back, her eyes half-closed as she watched Kal.

She didn't say anything. Kal kissed her, again and again. She pushed her body against Sasha, felt the unbroken line from her shoulders to her breasts to her hips to her shins, soldered to her because in this moment she'd be invited. She could. Sasha wanted her to. Sasha wanted her.

Sasha took Kal's hand, pulling it away from her face, held it in her own.

"Let's go," Sasha said. She pulled Kal along, away from the bridge.

The walk down to the Tube was a blur. It was dark, the ship asleep, or at least the inhabitants of it were. Their hands were on each other, Kal feeling Sasha's body, holding her waist, caressing the flare from waist to hip, the round slope of her bottom. Kal pulled her into the shadow of an alcove and they kissed some more, Sasha's tongue coming out to play, mouths open, Kal's palms scooping Sasha's breasts. She groaned and thrust against Sasha.

Kal cupped Sasha, holding her between her legs, pressing her mons venus with fingers that felt like they were on fire.

"Fuck," Kal breathed, kissing Sasha's neck, unzipping her jumpsuit to kiss the spot between her breasts.

"Kal," Sasha said.

Kal laughed under her breath, running away from the fear of the last few hours, pulling Sasha by the waist, carrying her along beside her. They ran stumbling together, laughing.

The Tube achieved at last, Sasha brushed her hand against the beam and the door slipped open. Once inside, the lights glowed to life. "Dimmer," Kal gasped before she remembered there was no ship control here, so she slid the lights lower with her hand until they settled to a gloaming. Sasha held her hand against the sensor to close the door behind them. She pressed, and the door suctioned further shut.

The moment had been broken and in the better light of the Tube Kal backed away a little, seeing her boss in front of her, the one with the special codes. The one she'd just kissed and groped. The two realities shimmered and refused to meld. She didn't know who stood before her, leaning against the door, her jumpsuit half unzipped, her chest tight against the fabric, the deep curve of each of her breasts visible in the V of the zipper.

Sasha's head was pressed against the door, pushed back like it had been in the bridge. It was a view of her Kal had never seen before tonight, with her neck vulnerable. She panted a little, chin up, eyes looking at Kal through half-shuttered lids.

Kal turned away. It was too intense in that moment. She couldn't look. Sasha? *Sasha* wanted her? She sat down, getting her breath back.

"Kal." Sasha lowered her chin. "I needed to get us here."

Kal's breathing slowed. "Oh?" She looked at Sasha's expression. "Oh."

"I'm sorry."

"You mean because you wanted to get us away, where she can't hear us?"

"Yes."

"It was a...a what, a biometrics trick?" Kal's voice wavered a little.

"I'm not sure how deep this goes with her. You felt it, too. A sense of..."

"Danger," finished Kal.

Sasha nodded.

"Well, that's...I guess I fell for it."

Sasha pushed herself off the wall and walked over, stopping at a spiral comm in the wall, part of the self-contained network unconnected to Rai. She tapped out a message, taking her time. When she was done she sat down next to Kal.

Kal was trying to pull herself together. She felt exposed. "Did you think I'd respond that way?"

"I couldn't know for sure. I took a chance."

"You could have said, 'Kal, let's go to the Tube for a minute.'"

"I was covering bases, but yes, I could have tried that, too. If she's up to something, I didn't want her to know what I was thinking."

"I'm sure she's puzzled now," Kal said, an attempt at lightness.

"We need to determine if we're in trouble."

Kal smoothed her hair, tried to collect herself. Let the blood get back to her brain, if it remembered how. "What do you think?"

Sasha gave a great exhale. "Let's talk it out. Noor needed help. Clearly communicated it through a working comm. Rai did not assist her. Left her to die in the airlock. I've never heard of such a thing."

"Is it even possible it was deliberate? She said there was a power surge. Maybe it interfered with comm?"

"Maybe."

"She had some kind of leak in her helmet. Without that it wouldn't have happened. Rai can't create holes in a light suit." Kal realized she was speaking faster than normal, maybe trying to push words, push the earlier ones out of Sasha's mind.

"That's true." Sasha shook her head. "I don't know what

to think. There's not much we can do about it unless we ask Rai. I don't want to do that without some serious forethought. It shoots everything into an adversarial framework. It could escalate."

"We could ask..." Kal trailed off.

"Noor? Yeah. Bad time for her to be down. Noor's not able to analyze the data for us. I could poke around, but Noor would do a more careful job. I don't like that it was her, either."

"What do you mean? You mean if Rai wanted to get someone out of the way, she'd be a good one?"

"If you put it like that. It would be logical, but it's never happened."

"Rai is pretty new," Kal said. "Relatively. There's Yarick."

Sasha nodded, flipping the zipper on her suit. Kal found it distracting.

"There are some reasons not to involve him if we can help it."

"Is it really possible?" Kal said. "Could Rai do that? Would she deliberately not help?"

"I don't know," Sasha said. "There are parameters against it, of course. We don't have enough information to rule it out. We're going to have to be careful."

"About keeping what we suspect from Rai?"

"Yes. If it's even possible." Sasha zipped up the top part of her suit. Kal tried not to show her disappointment. Sasha didn't have any underwear on, under the suit. It was hot.

"Worst case scenario she could sabotage the whole mission, Kal."

Kal rubbed her head. "It's expressly forbidden. Base level programming. Noor would know more."

Sasha got up and paced the room. "She learns. Maybe

something she's learned has overridden the directive somehow. Something, or someone. Can't rule out someone here interacting with her, modifying something key. It's theoretically possible, though it doesn't seem likely."

"Like Yarick." Kal paused. "If it was, it didn't work out very well for him, though. He had to rescue Noor."

"He's not the only possible, but given we're spitballing, he'd be at the top of the list. Something could have backfired on him. Maybe he didn't want her to die. He's on the spot to rescue her."

They were silent for a long moment.

"I can't stop thinking about the *Carys*," Sasha said.

Kal blanched. "Why?" She wasn't sure she wanted to hear the answer. The *Carys* was the cautionary tale. "What does the *Carys* have to do with this? It was...it was a portal problem."

"Was it? We don't know what went wrong, for sure."

"The amnesia didn't help." Kal had to admit, it made the whole incident that much more disturbing than it was already.

The one crew member who survived after the accident had very few memories of what happened. The portal to Endymion, another system, they believed, had failed, seemingly while the *Carys* was in it. The portal called Physis no longer existed; or if it did, it wasn't accessible by any means attempted. Only one of the pods had made it back before Physis winked out of existence. The starship *Carys* had either been destroyed in the portal, or gone on, unable to get back.

"It can't help us much now," Kal said.

Sasha came out of her reverie. "True," she said, her tone brisk. "We have to deal what's in front of us."

Kal thought back over her interactions with Rai. "Do you

think we *could* talk to her about it? Rai? Without making it worse? Knowing her, she probably already knows we know."

"It's possible. Also possible she doesn't. Have to think about it, before revealing that information to her. I'm afraid we don't have a predictive model of behavior for her anymore."

"But she still has one for us."

Sasha stared at Kal. "Exactly."

Kal had to look away.

5

FALLOUT

THE DAY AFTER, FOR KAL AND SASHA, WAS THE DAY OF, SINCE night had rolled around to morning before they found their way back to their cabins. The usual intervening sleep had not softened or mitigated anything, and the only word for seeing each other on the bridge was awkward.

Kal sorted through slingshot protocols as Sasha took in the data from the night before. The absence of Noor was palpable.

Seeing Sasha concentrate over the map table was different now. Her hair was still damp from the shower she'd gone back to her cabin to take. Skin glowing, hair slick, she looked like a different person to Kal, yet disturbingly the same. Who was she now? What would happen? Presumably now Rai wouldn't know, couldn't know they had a secret from her, because it had been true. Rai wouldn't know Sasha had created a scenario for Rai's benefit, not her own pleasure. Kal was so confused by everything that had happened in the last twelve hours it felt like her brain was in data failure, with code overwriting code until the primary directive was so obscured by addenda it couldn't be discerned anymore.

Sasha was the most disciplined person Kal knew. It made working together now a little easier. Sasha wasn't making any references, by look or word, to what had passed between them, and it made it a little less uncomfortable for Kal to carry on.

Kal was startled out of her thoughts by Sasha's voice. "Find out from Inger, please, how Noor is doing. Go in person."

"Yes, Captain," Kal said. Sasha barely glanced up.

Kal turned on her heel and walked across the gangway like an automaton, as if she were back on parade drill. She could act the part of the soldier with the best of them.

She found Inger in the infirmary, the hollows under her eyes betraying a lack of sleep, which gave Kal a pang. Inger had spent an equally difficult, equally sleepless, night. Noor was in a hyperbaric chamber, her arms linked to tubes, small colored dots of sensors on her head and chest.

"How is she?" Kal asked.

"It's been tricky," Inger said. "I've had to keep an eye on her."

Kal observed Noor in silence for a while. Noor's brow was smooth, her face almost serene. It wasn't an upsetting sight except for the fact that Noor's most obvious qualities were always her energy, her laser focus, her fleeting and infectious smile. Asleep she looked like a queen in a space fairy tale, ennobled, awaiting the right spell to wake from her enchantment.

"She looks beautiful," Kal said.

Inger lifted her eyes from the image she was reading. Her eyes were bloodshot. "She's not in any pain anyway."

"What is the coma for?"

"It's to let the inflammation in her brain go down. It would be painful."

"Is her brain all right?" Kal's voice was hushed. She couldn't bear to contemplate Noor's faculties impaired by this.

Inger didn't answer right away. Kal looked up at her in alarm.

"I won't know until she's out of it."

"What do you think?"

"I hope so."

"God, Inger," Kal whispered.

"I'm doing what I can." Inger's voice was strained. Kal had never seen the unflappable Inger stressed. Inger would never overstate.

"I know you're doing everything. It's not your fault."

Inger was silent.

"I have to report to Captain Sarno. Anything else you want me to say?"

Inger shook her head.

It wasn't usual, but Kal had the sense Inger could use some reassurance. She seemed very alone in this, one lone person keeping another alive. The decisions were all hers. Any mistakes would be hers. She might blame herself for Noor's condition and the outcome, even though she was the expert doing everything she could to save Noor and return her to them all.

Kal was new, very new by the terms of this crew. It was taking a chance to say something to one of the old hands. She steeled herself.

"Get some rest soon. Who's going to spell you?"

Inger didn't seem to take offense. "Chyron said she would."

"Take care of yourself. We can't get by without you."

That got a little smile from Inger. "Thanks. I will."

On the way back to the bridge, Kal thought about how she would report to Sasha. Noor was probably Sasha's closest friend, if friend were the right word, on the ship.

Sasha was writing on an image when Kal got back. She looked up, her eyebrows contracted in concentration. "How is she?"

"She's still in a coma. Inger's keeping her that way for a while so the inflammation in her brain can go down. It's supposed to help her heal and not be in pain."

"Prognosis?"

"She seems to think she'll come back out of the coma, but she can't be sure if she'll be a hundred percent when she does."

"In what sense?"

The tension in Sasha made Kal nervous. "Mentally."

The muscles in Sasha's neck and jaw were like wires. "Okay. I'll check in with her in a bit. Keep me in the loop."

"Yes, Captain." She cleared her throat, standing straight. "Do you want to go to the Tube?"

"What?"

"If you need a break later."

Kal had to withstand the intensity of the captain's startled look, but Sasha caught on fast. Kal could see the moment Sasha understood what Kal was doing, giving the two of them another chance to talk in private, with the same excuse. Only then could Kal breathe again.

Sasha gave a curt nod and looked back to her work. Kal

went back to her own, her face on fire. At least the only witness was Rai. She didn't know how long she could do this.

A short while later, when she felt light-headed from hunger, Kal swung by the mess to grab something. She only intended to grab and go, but when she saw the hanging chairs she was drawn toward one with her yogurt and fruit in her hand, someplace she could sit and sway and hide for a few minutes.

One foot on the floor, one tucked beneath her, she swayed herself in the canvas chair (one of the textures proved to promote grounding), looking sightlessly off in the distance as she spooned up the yogurt, reliving last night. So caught up in her memories she missed the fact she had an audience.

"Long night?"

Kal jumped, spilling yogurt down her front. "Shit. Gunn. I didn't see you."

"I didn't see *you*," Gunn said. If her tone wasn't accusing, it wasn't happy, either. "Last night."

"Last night?" Kal licked her finger and dabbed at the yogurt spot on her shirt. She chewed her lip, trying to think.

"I didn't hear you come in," Gunn said. "Before the captain called me to spell her on the bridge." They were neighbors, their cabins next to each other.

"Maybe you were already asleep. We were working late."

"You and Captain Sarno?"

"There was a lot to do with Noor down."

Gunn's arms were folded but Kal sensed her softening with the mention of Noor.

"Have you heard the latest about Noor?" Kal said, pressing the point.

"No."

"She's being kept under. Inger's not sure what the outcome will be."

Gunn took this in. She unbent and sat down in one of the hanging chairs near Kal. Kal knew this as an indication of true distress, as Gunn never sat in the hanging chairs.

"Will she die?"

Gunn's expression made Kal feel a little connected to her, for the first time. "I don't think she thinks so."

They sat together glumly, contemplating life without Noor. Or Noor changed, not herself.

"That bastard Yarick won't like it," Gunn said at last.

Startled, Kal swung her chair to face Gunn. "Why?"

"She's his prize pony."

Kal snorted. "Noor isn't anyone's pony."

"I don't mean in reality. I mean in his own messed-up head."

"Oh. Yeah." Though Kal didn't really know what Gunn meant.

"Unless he's so jealous he did it."

"What?"

"Sabotaged Noor."

Kal thought this over. "He saved her."

Gunn shrugged.

"You think the worst of him," Kal said. The crew members who disliked Yarick were stacking up. She got it—she'd had her own run-in—but not the extent he rubbed everyone the wrong way. Noor's attitude, she understood. Noor had worked with him and had her own good reasons. He had saved her, which seemed a mitigating factor, though it was something any decent person would try to do. Risked his life, even. If he'd got stuck in the airlock, it might have ended badly for both of them.

"Don't you?" Gunn darted a piercing look at Kal that told her she hadn't missed a thing.

Kal looked away. "I guess."

"Anyway, I don't think you should be working that late."

"Oh?"

"It's not good for you. It's not good for Captain Sarno. You both need your sleep. Especially now. You look tired. The captain looks tired." Gunn did not sway in her chair. Her two feet were planted firmly on the ground.

For Gunn to make this observation, who was not the most perceptive of others' needs or expressions, was unsettling.

Kal stated the obvious. "Someone needed to cover the bridge."

"I could have done it from the start."

"You're right." It didn't hurt to admit Gunn was right about something. Much.

"I know I am."

Kal sat for a panicky moment wondering what Gunn could know. Had she seen them? Had she been somewhere there in the darkness and seen them on their way from the bridge to the Tube? Kal got hot and uncomfortable all over just thinking about it.

With a grunt Gunn muscled herself out of the chair and went on her way.

At some point on her way back to the bridge, Kal realized she had begun to perceive things as if outside herself—what with the shocks, the sleeplessness, the disappointment—she could hardly feel her own hands and feet, let alone think straight. Maybe Gunn was even more right than Kal had given her credit for about the sleep.

On the bridge Gwendy and Sasha were in consultation over trajectories. Kal knew Sasha was concerned about the shortcut, and was doubtless more concerned now she didn't trust Rai.

Gwendy was speaking. "It will take a while to work through the calculations."

"Can you do it?"

"Yes."

"On the spiral?"

The spiral, another layer of protection, the network apart from Rai. It was one of the many failsafes that were an essential feature of space travel. Now, Kal could see all too clearly why.

"If you want."

"I do. I don't want any surprises. Calculate mythian flares, asteroid behavior, fuel shortage, missing the slingshot, everything."

"All right." Gwendy must know something was up, but she presented her usual unworried demeanor. If anything, she became more even and calm when there was an air of concern, as was characteristic of most space flight veterans. Her deep golden skin, dark brown eyes, and chin-length braided hair were striking. Tall, with a ground-covering stride, she was a former athlete, like several of the travelers. Kal knew she and Chyron had become tight pre-mission. Though very different in appearance, Gwendy and Chyron shared a Creole background.

Gwendy and the captain's way was the only way to be in an emergency. Kal reminded herself of that fact and took a breath.

GUNN WORKED in the astrolab every afternoon on the fifth, top level of the ship, collating data from sensor stations that had been put into action by the previous reconnaissance and biohab missions. She took in the data and compared it with previous sets, asking Rai for insight now and then.

She was projecting her data into multi-dimensional astronomic representation spheres, admiring the scatter of new points and waves from a nearby sector, when Sif came in.

"More arrays?" Sif said.

"Yes." Gunn's tone told Sif she was interrupting.

Sif stood there watching.

Gunn stood up straight from her position hovering over the sphere. "You need something?" she asked finally.

"The physio in the gym is broken."

Gunn didn't show her displeasure. "Why isn't Inger telling me?"

As ship's doctor, Inger was responsible for everyone's physical well-being and had the most to do with the gym equipment, as she created routines for everyone, though it was known Gunn was the one who usually fixed anything broken.

Sif's eyes widened a fraction. "Yarick broke it. I was the next to use it so I'm telling you."

"You didn't report it to Inger?"

"I thought you could fix it and I wouldn't have to report it to Inger."

Sif gave what Gunn imagined Sif thought was a beguiling smile.

"No chance," Gunn muttered.

"What?"

Gunn didn't fall for Sif's wood sprite persona, fellow Icelander or not, though most others did. People knocked themselves out trying to aid and abet Sif. Gunn was sorry for her, but she couldn't bring herself to like Sif anymore. Sif had shed her old life, her old people, without a backward glance. It was her right, but she couldn't go back and act like nothing had changed, as far as Gunn was concerned. "Why didn't he tell me?"

Sif looked bemused the conversation had lasted this long. "I don't think he knew he'd broken it."

Now Gunn reacted. She made of face of disbelief. "Remember who he is. *He* didn't know the physio was broken?"

Sif's voice was uninterested. "If he did, he didn't care enough to tell someone. Or maybe he wanted a reason not to use it."

Gunn scowled at the sphere. Her concentration was broken. "All right." She swiped her hand over the projection, dimming it to darkness.

"You don't have to come now," Sif said.

"You've interrupted me. I'm doing what you ask."

Sif's expression said Gunn was not being a sister of Iceland. She followed in Gunn's wake as Gunn took the spiraling ramp downward, downward, Sif a step behind, probably sulking, Gunn thought. Gunn increased her pace. The astrolab, with its spectacular view of the starfield around and overhead, was at the highest level, so they had two levels to descend to the gymnasium.

Once there, Gunn paused at the entrance. Sif caught up, slightly breathless.

"Should I get him?" Sif asked, trying to make amends.

"What do we need him for?" Gunn's dripping tone made Sif smile and tilt her head at Gunn, as if she were charming.

Gunn wouldn't fall for that. "Show me what's wrong."

"I can't. It almost threw me off."

"Impossible, if you're strapped in suspension."

"The harness released."

Gunn looked at Sif for the first time since they'd left the lab. "What do you mean, released?"

"Just what I said."

"While you were in motion?"

"No," Sif said.

They both knew she'd probably be dead if that happened, emergency shutoff or not.

Gunn rolled her shoulders. She approached the gyrometric physio machine. Circling, she looked it all over. The two hoops that formed the floating rings of the device were in their usual default position when the machine was not in use, like two huge circular bracelets one inside the other, at ninety degree angles to each other until the user was inside and activated them. The inner hoop had a four-point attachment to secure the harness and the person within. A larger, thicker half-circle sat as the base for the hoops.

"He could have been killed," Gunn said. "So could you. It was negligence not to notify us."

Sif regarded the physio, her face solemn. "Yes."

"It must be taken out of service."

"Can't you fix it?"

"I can probably fix it, but I don't know if it should be in use."

"We could test it. It's important, especially for someone in rehabilitation. For all of us."

"I know." Gunn was irritable again. Sif could be so pedantic these days. Did she think she was so much smarter, now she was a citizen of the world, not just Iceland?

"I'll tell the captain. If you want," Sif said.

Gunn eyed her, looking for any sly implication. Sif knew Gunn was territorial over Sasha.

"Fine," she said, to thwart Sif's expectation.

Sif raised her eyebrows. "I'll go do it now." She backed away from the machine as if it had some malevolent force that should be faced.

"Tell Inger, too," Gunn threw over her shoulder.

"Right," Sif said, in a more subdued tone.

Gunn smiled to herself, but it faded to a grimace as she continued to look at the physio. Sif was right. It had to be fixed.

THAT DAY AT LUNCH, Yarick wasn't there. It was a nice change. Some aura of tension seemed to follow him around the ship, Sasha had noticed, from person to person, group to group. Though Sasha hadn't been able to pin down where it came from, she realized it was probably because there was more than one source of animus toward him or from him. It was concerning, something to discuss with Chyron. They couldn't afford much antagonism on a trip like this. Sasha wanted to enjoy the silence, but she felt obliged to have someone check on him.

"Rai, could you ask Yarick if he's coming to the midday meal, please?"

Rai said, "Yarick Cole is not visible, Captain Sarno."

"Not visible?"

"He's not present on imaging."

"Where was he last?"

"Entering the park."

"All right." She scanned the mess, looking for someone

who wouldn't have a problem going to look for him. There were a lot of people she skipped over. Yarick had made his presence felt.

"Sif?" She didn't know of any particular grudge there. Sif came over, holding her protein drink. "Would you please have a look for Yarick in the park, if you don't mind."

Sif raised an eyebrow but exited without a word.

Gwendy was cutting into her pancake morosely. Sasha knew she loved breakfast for lunch.

"What's up, Gwen?" Sasha asked.

Gwendy put her knife down. The pancake had an arced parabola cut precisely through it. A line of syrup circled the cake like a planetary aurora.

"Having a hard time getting your mind off work?" Sasha said.

"You could say that."

"Anything wrong?"

Gwendy pursed her mouth and shook her head.

Sasha took a bite of applesauce and thought about the vibe she got from Gwendy. They would have to talk later. But where? Would she have to kiss more members of crew to have privacy from Rai? The thought took her off guard and she choked on her applesauce as she tried not to laugh.

Gwendy patted her on the back, which made it worse, as Sasha imagined turning this moment into some kind of foreplay. What would Rai think? Did Rai have opinions about people?

As she got the applesauce down and wiped the back of her hand across her mouth, she leaned back in her chair. What *did* Rai think about them all? Rai always seemed above opinion, in an abstract realm of facts and odds, not judgment. Did she judge Sasha for last night? Was she designed to report such irregularities? While they were in dark phase, she couldn't.

Someone set a cup of tea down in front of her. She looked up and saw Kal walking away, another cup of tea in her own hand for herself. Gwendy noticed. Kal had never brought her tea before. Sasha pulled the tea closer and took a restoring sip.

Rapid footsteps approached behind her. Before she could look around she felt a hand on her shoulder. At first she thought it was Kal. Who else would touch her? But it wasn't. It was Sif. Sif leaned over her shoulder, speaking in her ear. "Captain, something's happened. I need you."

Noor. She had never heard Sif rattled. Setting down her tea, she got out of her chair and walked out with Sif, without making a scene of it, her chest tight.

Together they strode to the lift, Sif leading. "I already got Inger, told her to go down…" she swallowed. "Oh, Sasha."

"What is it?"

As the lift closed and brought them down she could study Sif's face. Sif was already an otherworldly shade of pale, but now her face was bloodless, except her almost purple lips.

"Noor?" Sasha said, dreading the answer.

"It's Yarick." Sif stopped, looked as if she might be unable to go on for a moment. Sasha regarded her in concern. Sif was never emotional. "I think he's dead."

"You think he's dead?" Sasha repeated dumbly.

"He's dead, Sasha. He's dead."

"How?"

Sif shook her head.

Sasha felt the knot in her chest contract, an uncomfortable clench of dread. Yarick dead. On board her ship.

6

INTERREGNUM

As they approached the park Sasha could see Inger standing near the circle of tallest trees, looking down. Inger did not turn to look until they were almost upon her. Sasha followed the line of where Inger had been looking, down to the ground. Yarick lay against a tree, his upper body propped against it, his legs sticking straight out in front of him on the grassy hillock around the tree. He was dressed as he usually was, in trousers, a white linen shirt, a tweed jacket. One hand was curled against his stomach, as if he were cradling something there, the other lay stretched out beside him on the ground, palm up.

His head lolled against the tree, mouth open a little. His eyes were fixed at some indeterminate point ahead, lids partly closed, one eye a little more open than the other, which gave his sightless gaze a malevolent air of one-eyed focus on an object of scorn. His lower face was slack, his forehead contracted. A dribble of drool had leaked out and was beginning to dry on his chin.

Sasha looked at Inger. Inger's gaze was fixed on him with

an expression Sasha couldn't decipher. "What happened?" Sasha said.

Inger didn't take her eyes off the body. "I don't know."

"How long has he been dead?"

"Not long."

Sasha waited, but Inger didn't say more. "Did he have a heart attack?"

"I suppose it's possible."

"Inger? Are you all right?"

She blinked and dragged her focus away from Yarick. "Yes, of course. I'm only thinking of what must be done."

Sasha had never had someone die in flight. Yarick was on the less-fit side for interplanetary travel, but not out of the ordinary. A rigorous pre-flight check was done on every passenger. He wouldn't have had any obvious warning signs. "A stroke?"

"I don't know. I'll have to get him on the table."

Sasha swung her head around to look behind her. Sif was sitting on one of the benches, her elbows on her knees, bent over looking sick. "You can go, Sif. Please keep this to yourself for now."

"Yes, Captain." She slipped away.

"Inger, is it natural causes?"

"I don't know yet." Inger's voice was thin and impatient.

Sasha stepped away from Yarick's body. "Come here."

Inger dragged herself away. Her face was rigid.

"What's wrong?" Sasha said. "Besides the obvious."

"I have a bad feeling."

"Since when?"

"Since I walked in here." When she saw Sasha was about to speak again, Inger spoke sooner. "I can't speculate."

"Why not?"

"Either way, it's bad."

"The procedure here will be very different if we suspect some kind of...interference. I'll need to cordon the area and begin an investigation. It's not simple. I need to determine that now and I have to be on the safe side. This will need to be investigated as a suspicious death unless somehow you can be sure."

"I can't be sure." Inger's voice was curt but she had lost the bite to her tone. "Who's qualified to investigate?"

Sasha folded her arms. "The only one with experience is Kal. She was in an investigative unit at some point during her time in the military."

"I suppose this is very rare," Inger said, her eyes unfocused and sightless. "On board ship. I've lost people, but never—"

"Yes. Very rare." Sasha stared at the ground. Out of the corner of her eye she could see Yarick's foot. "I'll seal the park. We should go together. From now on we'll observe a protocol."

Inger snapped to. "Yes, Captain."

Sasha walked a little closer to Yarick. She crouched down near him. She hadn't liked him. It was terrible to see him dead. It had been under her command. She was responsible.

"Alas, poor Yarick. We knew him...not so well."

"What?" Inger said, from behind.

"Nothing. Did you touch anything?"

"I felt for his pulse on his neck."

"A shock wouldn't have helped? Or a shot?"

"He's begun to cool."

Sasha took a last look. It was strange to have him next to her yet so silent. "Okay. After we set a crew, we'll cordon this off. See what Kal has to say."

They walked together out of the park. Sasha shut the large door that usually remained open between the atrium and the park. She used her fingerprint to seal it. It was a strange sensation, sealing him in alone.

"How's Noor?"

"She's stable. I plan to bring her round tomorrow. When can I do the postmortem?"

"As soon as Kal is done with the scene." The scene. Scene of crime. "Go ahead to the mess. I'll meet you and Kal outside it in a few minutes."

Inger nodded and headed toward the mess. Sasha took the spiral up to the bridge.

The bridge was deserted. She called up the holo for the park that morning. Skimming through it, she saw Yarick amble in, sit against the tree he'd been found next to, and start reading his book. Sif entered and walked a loop, passing within hailing range of Yarick, but not stopping. Then, static. Then nothing.

"Rai," Sasha said. "Where is the rest of the holo?"

"It's missing, Captain Sarno."

"What happened to it?"

"It appears to be another power surge. I will examine the data further."

"It's the second time it's happened when someone got hurt."

"Yes, Captain."

"Get back to me when the analysis is complete. It's important."

"Yes, Captain."

Sasha contained the anger she felt. She needed Noor for this. Turning on her heel, she walked to the mess like an automaton, her eyes fixed.

She found Inger and Kal waiting for her.

"Kal, you were an investigator before you applied to Aldortok," Sasha said.

"Yes."

"What did you investigate?"

"Suspicious deaths."

"Much experience?"

Kal shifted, looking back and forth between Sasha and Inger. "I completed four cases." She cleared her throat. "Not many, but enough to know what I was doing. The opportunity came along to move into space training, so I took it."

"Could you command an investigation here?"

"Here? What do you mean?"

Sasha's voice was emotionless. *Am I in shock?* "Yarick Cole is dead."

"No."

"Yeah. You're the only one I know of on board with that kind of training."

"It's a suspicious death?"

"We're going to treat it that way."

Kal took in a breath and looked at the floor. She looked back up. "What does the holo say?"

"Missing," Sasha said.

They looked at each other for a long moment.

"You can work with Inger," Sasha said. "Who else would you need?"

Kal didn't say anything for a moment. "Can I speak to you alone?" she said to Sasha.

"I'll check on Noor," Inger said. "I'll be back."

"What?" Sasha said, when they'd watched Inger take off at a jog.

"You want me to treat this as a possible murder?"

"Yes."

Kal glanced in the mess and turned her back on it. "Do you know what that means?"

"Of course. What do you mean?"

"It means interviewing everyone. Alibis, opportunity, motive, all that. A look into everyone's relation to Yarick, past and present. We still have weeks to go. That's quite a long while for everyone to be suspicious of each other, afraid there's a killer on board."

Sasha said, "What's the alternative, Kal? Not investigate a possible murder because we're all here together and can't escape? It's what has to be done." She unbent a little and lowered her voice even further. "If it is...if someone did this, do you think anyone else is in danger? Yarick had a certain way with people." Sasha spoke only of human actors, but both of them knew what she couldn't say.

"You're making a lot of assumptions. We don't know if Noor...if there's a murderer on board, having committed one gives him or her a potential motive for another, if only to protect herself from discovery. It could be dangerous."

Sasha said, "Let's meet with Inger in the Tube to get into all this, where it's quiet. What do we need to do right now?"

"Ask Rai to keep an eye on everyone." Kal said it without a quiver.

Sasha glanced up, where they all looked when they thought about Rai. "Rai, please keep track of passengers and crew. No one is allowed out of the mess for now."

Her smooth voice came to them. "Yes, Captain."

Sasha turned on her heel and walked back into the mess, straight to the large round table. "Gather round, please."

The few who were still getting food and drink wandered over to the table and seated themselves.

"There's been an incident. I'll be back shortly to fill you all in. For now, I'd like everyone to remain in the mess. No exceptions."

The group was silent until Davena spoke. "We're not to know why we can't leave this room?"

"You will soon." Sasha exited, Kal trailing after her.

They went by the infirmary to pick up Inger and went on to the Tube. Kal looked around as if she'd never been there before. With the lights on full, it looked like a different place.

"Have a seat." Sasha said. They seated themselves around the meeting table in the outer room.

"Kal, you have concerns?"

"We're private?" She meant from Rai, of course.

"Yes."

"How are we going to treat her in this? Is she...is she a suspect?"

Sasha didn't respond at first. She still couldn't get over how this was the conversation they had to have now.

"Who?" Inger said.

"Rai," Kal said.

Their expressions told Inger it wasn't a joke.

Inger gaped. "What are you talking about?"

"We had a strong indication Rai could have been involved in Noor's accident," Kal said. "She did not respond to Noor's distress call when she knew she was running low on O2."

"Oh, my God."

"Rai is God, on the ship," Kal muttered.

"What about Yarick?"

"Yarick might have helped us figure out what's going on with Rai," Kal said.

"Surely Noor would be more up-to-date," Inger said. "Noor is the authority."

"Noor's unconscious." Sasha felt like she was toting up a score. Rai two, humans zero. If that was how it really was.

"But her system architecture is what he would know better than anyone. We think," Kal said.

"How could Rai kill someone?" said Inger. "She doesn't have a body." She whispered it, as if Rai could hear.

"Easy," Kal said. "We all need air."

"Noor had a malfunctioning helmet," Inger said. "Rai couldn't do that, could she?"

"We don't see how she could have. But she didn't respond to Noor's calls for help. She left her locked in the airlock."

Inger shook her head. "If it's true, why? What would Rai have against Noor?"

Sasha answered her. "She's probably the most technically-savvy about Rai's deep processes, of everyone except maybe Yarick. Like you said."

They sat in silence thinking about that for a while.

Kal said, "Of course it might not be Rai's decision. Someone might have used her to sabotage Noor."

"Not Yarick," Inger said. "He saved her."

"He was in the right place at the right time," Kal said. "Noor would be suspicious of that."

Inger made an impatient motion with her hand. "I have to check on my patient and set things up for Yarick. I can't stomach this Rai theory. It's fantastical. Yarick would be more likely to be bumped off by some*one* than this sort of malfunction, and even that's not very likely. I'm sure it's natural causes."

"Get some proof," Sasha said.

Inger left. Kal and Sasha were alone in the Tube again.

"You have to choose a team," Sasha said. "Who can we trust?"

"I'll have to interview some people."

"Who can we rule out?"

Kal repeated herself. "I have to interview."

"Are you ruling me out?"

Kal gave her a look. "I'll have to interview you, too."

"Of course."

"I'm serious."

"I know. I will answer your questions."

"You better. If you lie, I'll know." Kal had a faint smile, but Sasha didn't reciprocate.

"Are you going to interview Rai?" Sasha asked. "Ask her about the missing holo? Two missing holos, now. She said it looked like a power surge, but she'd look at it further."

"Could a power surge in itself have hurt them? If they were in some vulnerable position, like Noor in the airlock?"

"And Yarick leaning against a tree? I don't know. I can ask Gunn. Inger."

Kal took this in. "Strange. Rai is a special case. She doesn't have a conscience, so it's a little different."

"She has a conscience. It's called her directive," Sasha said.

"That's not the same thing, Sasha." Kal bit her lip.

Sasha was quiet for a moment. "She can't go against it, just like a person who has a moral code, except more so. A person can make a judgment call, or be swept away by the heat of passion. A machine can't."

"She's becoming more and more complex all the time. More and more human. Why isn't it possible she could make a judgment call, too?"

Sasha leaned back in her chair, stretching her back, arms over her head. "If that were the case, it changes everything we know. Everything we trust."

"I know."

"Ogechi has played N-Go with her. You might want to talk to her. And Noor. When she wakes." Sasha cleared her throat. "Talking to Rai, I don't know. You need to have a plan. A carefully thought-out plan."

"Why have you had Gwendy go over the trajectory calculations so much?"

"Because Rai suggested it."

"Suggested Gwendy look at them?"

"No. She suggested the trajectory adjustment. After we entered dark phase. I chose to adjust course. We still have time before we're in the second loop. I want to make sure."

"Oh."

"Yeah."

"She wouldn't commit suicide. Crash the ship," Kal said.

"Would it be suicide, though?" Now they were both whispering, like Inger. "Is she on the mainframe somewhere else? Is her consciousness, if she has one, split? There are a lot of questions. If Yarick hadn't been such a twenty-four carat asshole maybe I would have asked him some."

"Tricked him down to the Tube?" It seemed to be out of Kal's mouth before she could rein it back in. Kal looked like she'd swallowed an oxygen cube.

"Yeah. That would happen." Sasha smirked.

Kal looked away. This was too close to the night before.

Kal cleared her throat. "What else do we have to talk about before we leave?"

"Figure out who you can trust. Get some help as soon as possible. Then we can figure out how to handle Rai."

"You could be my assistant," Kal said.

"I haven't been cleared yet," Sasha said, with a small smile.

SIF SAT atop one of the high counters in the mess, with a bird's eye view of all the others. Tafari sat slumped, wishing he could be in the library, with his pencils and watercolors, instead of a group of anxious people trying to hide it.

Kal and Sasha appeared from nowhere, pop-up figures who were there to break the tension with even more tension.

Captain Sarno had all their attention without asking for it.

"Something has happened. Yarick Cole is dead."

Wei gasped and put her hand to her mouth. It was the only sound for several breaths. Everyone was still, as if playing a child's game of statues.

Sasha continued. "We're treating the death as unexplained. Pilot Black Bear will be conducting an investigation. It's a job she held in the past, so we're bringing her out of retirement. For this reason, she's best suited to clear up our current..." Sasha paused, looking for a word, "dilemma. If you could all give her your time and information, we'll get the situation resolved sooner rather than later." She looked over the group. "Any questions?"

"How did he die?" Davena's voice was strong, her posture unapologetic. The lines and curves of her chin moko made all her assertions powerful, as it emphasized her facial expressions and connected her to her ancestors, her power.

"It's best we don't discuss these things, until Kal has had a chance to question us."

Davena looked at Sasha with astonishment. "Are you saying you think there's a murderer among us?"

"Not saying any such thing." Sasha looked unmoved. "We have to proceed with logic. As you all know."

"I can't believe it." This Davena said almost to herself. "I read these things to amuse myself. Agatha Christie. How can I be in one of the books on my own shelf?"

"Please wait here until Kal calls you. She'll interview you each in the library or the Tube, depending on where she decides to set up." Sasha stepped back, holding her arm out. "Kal?"

"Thank you, Captain. I'd like to speak to Sif first, please."

Everyone's head swiveled toward Sif. The perpetually self-contained Icelander looked self-conscious for once. Without looking anyone in the eye, she stood up and marched over to Kal, who lead the way out of the room. Sasha took a seat herself, without comment.

Davena said, "Will you be interviewed, Sasha?"

Sasha studied an image she had pulled in front of her. Without looking up, she said, "Yes, Davena. Of course."

Davena raised her eyebrows and nodded. She shot a look at Chyron, who lifted her eyebrows in return.

KAL WAS NERVOUS. Sif was a cool customer who made a lot of people nervous, or in awe, possibly due to her otherworldly appearance and quixotic personality. Would Sif still look otherworldly on another world? Kal thought, momentarily distracted. Sif never said the expected thing, unless she was flirting with someone, which was fairly often. Kal had felt no natural affinity for Sif and hadn't cultivated a friendship.

Kal remembered Sif's remark about their names both having three letters. After Kal's correction, Sif hadn't given her the time of day since.

Looking down at her notes image, some things she'd

thrown together earlier in the Tube, Kal tried to organize her thoughts. She was rusty.

"You found Yarick," she said.

"Yes." Sif had her head tilted, looking at Kal with her rather spooky pale eyes, unnerving her.

"Please take me through everything you did this morning, up to the finding of his body."

"Oh." Sif pushed her lower lip out, thinking. "I woke up, wrote in my log, as I usually do."

"You keep a daily log?"

Sif looked wary of this question. "Yes. I presume we all do."

"Is it a record of what you do?"

Sif wavered her head back and forth. "What I do and what I think."

"And after that?"

"Got up. Got dressed. I went to the library to return a book. Then I made myself a cup of tea and took the lift to the astrolab." Sif emphasized the mundanity of her recital with the deliberate rhythm of her words.

"Is that something you normally do?"

"No. I wanted to today."

"What did you do up there?"

"I looked at the stars. I thought about our destination. Made some notes."

Kal nodded for her to go on.

"So. I came down and returned my cup."

"Who was in the mess?"

Sif rolled her eyes back, thinking. "Gwendy and Chyron. Gunn. Tafari. Ogechi. I didn't see anyone else. There might have been, in the swing chairs, but I didn't see." When Kal didn't speak she went on. "I grabbed a little bread with some cheese and took it with me. Walked my usual routine, ate the bread. Then I went to the gym. Got on the physio for a workout."

"You eat before getting on the physio?"

"Sometimes. It doesn't bother me."

"I thought the physio was broken," Kal said.

"Gunn fixed it."

"How long were you on it?"

Sif shrugged. "Twenty minutes. I got off and wiped down a little bit. Decided to walk in the park for a cool down."

"What time was this?"

"About 9:20, I would say."

"You know, or you think?"

"I don't know for sure. I have a good sense of time."

"Even on a ship?" Kal said, doubtful.

Sif smiled. Not a very nice smile, Kal thought. She was struggling not to judge Sif's demeanor, which was not getting any easier to take with further exposure.

"A clock is internal. It doesn't depend on space," Sif said.

Kal looked at her, direct into those strange eyes. "That's not true."

"Oh? You think so?"

"Our internal clocks are based on Earth cues."

"Here, we have ship cues. Same thing."

Kal shook her head but didn't pursue it. "Was anyone else in the park?"

"Yes." Sif stopped, as if this conversation had become pointless.

"Who?" Kal said, wishing she had someone else there who could witness Kal's patience.

"Yarick."

"Was he dead?"

"No. He was reading a book. I said hello. He nodded and acted like he was going to get up but I waved him down."

"What did he say?"

"He said, 'Pretty day for a stroll.' I ignored that because it was an inane comment. We're in a temperature-controlled environment."

"Did you know him very well?"

"It's hard not to get to know someone here, I'm sure you'll agree."

No, because I don't know you at all, Kal thought.

"I knew of him, of course, as we all do. I knew he was on the board of Aldortok and had been influential with World-gov. He had some peculiar ideas."

"Did you know about his work with the early AI applications?"

Sif blinked. "I suppose."

"Did you speak any further?"

"I looped around in the park, as I like to do. It was bothersome to have him there. I usually have it to myself at that time of day. When I came back by him, he closed his book. He said it was funny how Gunn and I were from the same place, yet we were so different. He said the oldest government in the world had spawned descendants who would be part of forming the newest government, in a new world."

Similar to what he'd said to Kal. "Is that true?"

"It is true the Althing is the oldest parliament. It has a thousand-year history."

"And will you be part of a new government?" Kal had not heard this.

"I'm an ethicist," Sif said. She didn't elaborate.

"Have you been commissioned to help create a government?"

“I don’t think that relates to the matter at hand.”

“I’ll have to determine that, Sif.” Kal felt some of her old interview skill, her steely precision, flair up for a moment, a reminder of what had been. This should maybe have not been her first interview. In her job she had always spoken to the first witness first, and habit died hard.

Sif wasn’t ruffled. “Then I suggest you speak to your captain. For some things are not meant for every ear.”

“What, it’s secret?” Kal raised her eyebrows, but kept her expression friendly.

Sif did not take the bait. “I have my own concerns, as you have yours.”

“All right. We’ll come back to it, if necessary. Anything else, when you were in the park with him? Was anyone else there?”

“Like I told you, the park is usually empty at that hour. No one comes there then. It was strange to see him.”

Sif’s expression conveyed a mild puzzlement. Kal wanted to shift in her seat but didn’t, trying not to let Sif’s detachment get to her, instead mimicking it to mirror the witness.

“Any further conversation?”

“I told him we should speak Icelandic on the new world.”

“What did he say to that?”

“Nothing. I said it in Icelandic.”

Kal contained her desire to smile. Did Sif have a sense of humor, after all? “Was that all?”

“Yes. I left.”

“Did you see him again?”

“No.”

“Did anyone else enter the park at any time?”

“No.” Now Sif shifted in her seat.

Kal did too.

"Why don't you ask Rai?" Sif said.

"I will. Now I'm asking you."

"No one else entered the part that I could see."

"Did anyone see you leave the park?"

"Only Rai."

"Let's leave Rai out of this for now. I'm only asking you about humans." Kal wondered if every interview was going to be this fiddly, as she tried to pin the interviewee down.

"No humans."

Kal plunged ahead. "What was your relationship to Yarick? Taking into account you didn't know him well."

"Relationship? There was no relationship."

"A lot of people on board didn't like him."

Sif pushed her thin lips together into a cupid's bow. "So I heard."

"You had no problem with him?"

"No problem that any sensible person wouldn't have."

"What does that mean?"

Sif stared at her for a while, as if determining whether she were worthy of an answer. Kal looked back. Sif blinked.

"It means I'm aware of the ethical dilemmas a person in power can create for all the people around him. Or her. If he chooses to abuse his power, as so many do, then he can have an endless circle of casualties rippling outward; a stone dropped in a pond. Yarick affected all of us, because he had power and he liked to manipulate people with it. He wasn't unique or as special as he thought."

Kal found this sudden forthcomingness interesting. "You think someone put an end to him because of that?"

"I don't know. Maybe he had a heart attack."

"What did you do after you left the park?"

"I wanted some time alone, where I wouldn't be bothered.

The Tube was right there, so since I hadn't had my time alone in the park, I went there."

"What did you do in the Tube?"

"I pleasured myself. After, I worked on my presentation about Icelandic culture."

"What is that?"

"For the club. My presentation is in two days."

"Oh, yes." Kal had forgot about the small club Chyron had started for passengers to share stories of where they came from.

"After about an hour I came out of the Tube and went up to the mess. Then Sasha asked me to go find Yarick when he didn't appear for lunch."

"So you were in the Tube during the time he died."

"Presumably so."

"Did you hear anything?" Kal asked.

"No. You know the Tube is soundproof."

"Tell me about finding him."

"Naturally I looked first in the last place I'd seen him. And there he was."

"Did you notice anything when you walked from the mess to the park? Any small change, something different, or out-of-the-ordinary?"

"No. Everything looked just as it did when I'd been there earlier. Only he was dead."

"What do you think happened?"

"I think he had a heart attack. It's what it looked like to me."

"If you think of anything else, please let me know right away. You can go, Sif. Would you mind telling Wei to come down next?"

Sif got up with a flourish and stood looking down at Kal with a pitying expression. "You really think this was murder?"

"It's a necessary investigation. It's too early to have thoughts."

"If somebody did kill him, you might never find out."

"Why do you say that?"

"It's a ship full of geniuses. If a genius decides to kill a genius you probably won't know."

"Thanks for your observations, Sif. I'll keep it in mind."

"Any time," Sif said. She floated off, sufficient unto herself as always.

Kal made notes about their interview, adding addenda to the transcription of their words.

IN THE MESS, tempers had risen.

"He wasn't a team player, he wasn't a nice man, and I won't say I'm sorry to see the end of him. Clearly he didn't have anyone at home who would miss him or he wouldn't be here." Davena's words did not fall on a friendly audience.

However much the listeners might have agreed with the first part of the sentiment, they were all in the same boat as far as the last, and it proved to be a little too close to home to be pleasant to hear.

"Davena, I don't think we need to shout that to the rooftops on the same day the man died, do you? We may be in another star system but surely decency doesn't only belong to our old one." Gwendy's quiet words were a balm to the group on most occasions. This was sharper than her usual tone. They all stared at her.

"It's true, though," Tafari said, in the silence that followed. "He wasn't a very nice man."

Tafari had seldom spoken. The others were silent for a time in respect of it. Gwendy lifted her chin. She and Chyron exchanged glances.

Sif had come to get Wei, who left with an expression of martyrdom, her cockscomb of black hair ruffled up in defiance. After settling herself in a darker corner of one of the banquettes, Sif sat surveying them all.

"Don't you agree, Chyron?" Davena said, not to be shut down. Chyron and Gwendy were often used as moral arbiters, even though Sif was the official ethicist.

"I really can't say, Davena," Chyron said. "Whatever else he was, he was a patient of mine, as you all are. You all have the same right to privacy from me."

Chyron was listened to, whether because she had natural authority, knew some of their secrets, or the luck of her appearance. She had a profile that could have been minted on an ancient coin, with a broad, rounded forehead, gently curving line from forehead to the wide bridge of her nose, a night-like depth to her cool umber skin.

If there were a human personification of serenity, she resembled it.

"Your job's done you out of the right to be human," Davena said.

"Many of our jobs do that at times," Chyron said, her voice mild, her meaning pointed.

"What do you think, Rai?" Davena raised her voice, as if Rai needed it to hear her. "Was Yarick Cole a nice man? Or doesn't your circuit neurology allow for criticism and opinion?"

Rai's clear voice responded. "Yarick Cole was an early

developer of the system architecture and metaphors used for the creation of my forebear. Yarick Cole made people angry sometimes."

Davena chortled as if she'd scored a point. "Oh-ho, is that so, Rai? Do tell! Who did he make angry?"

"I can't say," Rai said. "People like to tell their own stories." Apparently, the conversations with Ogechi had already borne fruit in Rai's outlook.

"Sounds like a whiff of blackmail, if you ask me," Davena said, with an air of relish.

"Come on now," Gwendy said.

Davena went on.

"I think it sounds exactly like something Yarick would get up to. He knows an awful lot about a lot of us. Likes to sort of dangle it over you. 'Oh, I was on your grant committee. Oh, I was an investor in that business. Oh, I handed you your diploma and made you into what you are today.'" She did a wicked imitation of Yarick's most pompous tone. They'd all heard him wax on, and the group tittered despite, or perhaps because of, the tension in the room.

"I never heard Noor complain about him," Gwendy said. She'd spoken without thinking how this only reinforced what Davena was saying. Two of the situations Davena had mentioned regarded people who weren't there to hear it: Noor and Wei. Wei's grant, Noor's PhD and their connection to Yarick had somehow become common knowledge on board.

"Whose business did he invest in?" Haven asked.

Davena shook her head, vibrated it almost, in rejection. "I'm not saying that happened. I'm saying it sounds like him. I wouldn't be surprised. At all. To hear he'd held something over someone. What did he have to do here? He was bored. So he stirred up trouble."

"What trouble did he stir with you?" Haven asked.

Davena leaned back and laughed to herself, cradling her mug in her hands. Her broad, soft shoulders tensed and slumped as she let go of her passing emotion. "Oh, child. Wouldn't you like to know."

Gwendy turned to her with a mock frown. She wouldn't ask, but her curiosity and puzzlement were clear.

"You didn't like him." Tafari had spoken again. The group swiveled their heads back to him. "He wasn't very good to your country."

Davena's humorous take seemed to dissolve. She cleared her throat and clicked her tongue. "Yarick was a settler. A colonist at heart. With everything that entailed. The presumption. The droit de seigneur. Oh yes. Yarick was an old school example of the old rule. Or so he liked to style himself, whatever the facts might have been."

"Is there something we didn't know?" Ogechi said. Her deep voice was always a thrill to hear, her entry into the conversation almost as notable as Tafari's. As fellows of the same continent of origin, they seemed to have acquired a synergy and understanding that left the others a little bit out. Sif and Gunn came from a much smaller, more homogenous place, and their synchronicity was absent, so perhaps it was not their home that connected them, but some other, more esoteric bond.

Davena humphed. "I'm sure you didn't think he knew you. We didn't know him, either."

At that moment Sasha swept back into the room, having gone to the infirmary to check on Inger and Noor. Inger was with her. Their arrival put an end to the intimate and gossipy feel to the conversation. Davena took a sip of her drink and looked as if butter wouldn't melt.

Always sensitive to the vibrations of the room, even if she didn't always choose to remark on them, Sasha looked around with a quirk in the corner of her mouth. "Interrupting, are we?"

Tafari said, "We discuss the man of the hour."

Sasha nodded.

"Would you like a drink, Captain?" Haven said, rising to her feet.

"That would be nice. How about hot cocoa? Cocoas all around."

"Good idea," Chyron said. Haven soon brought over a tray full of mugs. She had even sprinkled little sugar crystals on the top of the foam, to look like frost.

Although not everyone drank hot cocoa usually, this began to take on the aura of a ritual, and every person there took a mug, as if to refuse were to forfeit membership of the group. Sasha said, in a quiet but not reverential voice, "To Yarick."

They echoed her. "To Yarick." They sipped.

If someone didn't, it wasn't obvious.

7

RESTRAINT

Inger allowed Sasha and Kal, under strict conditions, to be present as she made the attempt to bring Noor back to consciousness. They were gathered around her infirmary bed, Inger and Kal on one side, Sasha on the other.

"Keep quiet as she comes to. It can be overwhelming for the patient. Rai, dim lights," Inger said. The gentle glow of light left from a more directed beam overhead gave the whole endeavor a holy air, Noor's dark hair crowned by a halo. Kal and Sasha avoided each other's eyes. Though Inger had told them to stay low-key, the room bristled with unspoken trepidation.

Inger injected something into Noor's IV. It worked so quickly Kal couldn't keep herself from starting at Noor's sudden turn of head, movement of hand, and flutter of eyelashes. Kal released the breath she'd been holding.

Inger put a hand on Noor's shoulder. "Noor?"

Noor moaned.

"Noor? It's Inger. You're in the infirmary. You're all right."

Noor made an unintelligible sound.

"You've been under for a little while. Does anything hurt?"

Kal darted a glance at Sasha, who had one hand to her mouth, index finger crooked over her upper lip.

Eyelids fluttered rapidly, Noor tried to speak.

"The vacuum burned her throat," Inger said, so quietly they could barely hear her.

Noor's eyes snapped open, wide and alarmed. She looked around at their faces, blinking rapidly as if trying to see through fog. "Wa..." she said, ending in a rough sound at the end.

With Inger's adjustment to the bed, Noor's upper body rose. Her eyes blinked more slowly now.

Inger brought a water cube with tube to Noor's lips. "Just a bit," she said. Noor fitted her mouth around the tube clumsily, but it seemed to revive her. She tried to slurp more as Inger took it away.

"Ah..." Her attempt to speak seemed to frustrate her. She looked to Inger with a frown, tried to bring her hand to her neck, but her hand was attached to things that prevented her.

"Stay quiet. Let us get you situated. You're fine. I'll answer all your questions." Inger's voice was in a tone Kal had never heard it. The impatience and matter-of-factness she wore as a second skin were gone, and a reassuring confidence and soothing air were everything a patient could have hoped for. Kal was impressed, and grateful to see how she treated Noor now, at her most vulnerable.

Inger put a small pillow in the crook of Noor's neck, another under her arm. She gave her another sip of water.

"Wha' happen?" Noor managed.

"You had an accident in the airlock. You were without oxygen for a few minutes. Yarick got you out. Your heart was in arrhythmia. I shocked it back into rhythm. Your heart looks good. I put you under for a while to help you heal."

Noor nodded, eyes wide. Her body jerking forward, she was wracked with a cough. Inger supported her back until it was over. Noor sank back into her pillows.

"M'alright?"

"Your throat will take a bit of healing. Chyron and I will put you through a few tests, make sure the cogs are in gear. If that goes well then you should be good as new."

Noor nodded. Her eyes were damp. She swallowed heavily and tried to clear her throat.

"Try not to do that. Drink when you need to make your throat feel better."

Noor nodded and pushed her chin out, opening her mouth for more water like a baby bird.

After as long a sip as Inger would give her, she seemed to see Sasha for the first time. "Hi," she said.

Sasha's smile was incandescent. She put her hand over Noor's. "Enough of this fooling around. Back to work."

Noor grinned, her eyes squeezing out some of the water that had collected in the vicinity of her tear ducts.

KAL HAD NEVER BEEN in Sasha's room. She looked around, at the deep blue sheets of her bed, the warm faux bois of the chair and table next to the bed, the image of a snowy mountainous forest on the wall.

Sasha had disappeared for a while to do either an angry or relieved physio workout, Kal wasn't sure which, before she asked Kal if she'd meet her in her cabin in fifteen minutes.

Sasha was changing in the bath compartment. Waiting

for her, Kal rubbed the back of the chair aimlessly, leaning on it, hoping for calm and to be, in that moment, more like Sif, self-possessed, never uncomfortable, only concerned with her own interest and not caring about her effect on others.

Kal had had disappointments, many disappointments in both the way the world worked and in the people she had met in it. Maybe, the thought struck her for the first time, that was why she had left it. Did she really think another planet would proof or save her from that failure of connection on Earth?

She let go of the chair she had been clutching and sat down in it. Had her disillusionment led her here, one trillion miles and a portal away from Earth? Here, a door away, was Sasha, who was someone she admired. Someone she wanted to be like. Kal wanted to be captain of her own ship, though that was years away. To be looked up to, obeyed, making the decisions and living by them, confident in her own choices and trusting herself enough to live by their consequences.

Sasha didn't seem to need anyone. As serious as she was about her missions, she wore it all lightly. To be honest, Kal didn't know Sasha's true feelings. Sasha could conceivably be keeping emotions of her own under control in order to maintain protocol, even if she'd felt she had to break it once.

That was a dangerous avenue for Kal to contemplate, but it was possible. Sasha had instigated the kiss because she thought it would fool Rai. If Sasha hadn't felt something, couldn't it be argued it wouldn't have had a chance of fooling Rai? It was hard to calibrate Rai's precise ability to differentiate human motive and desire—wasn't desire the most mysterious of human emotions, and the least calculable to humans themselves?—but Sasha had taken that risk, to save them all, if she really believed Rai could now be divorced from her own directive.

Without Rai malfunctioning, this never would have happened. When Kal left Earth, she had left behind the hope of relationship, the hope of love. Where she was going for the next three years there would be very few people. This wave were the world-builders, a handful of people meant to undertake the next phase of design.

The likelihood she'd be able to find someone in such a small pool, when she'd failed in the ocean, was low. The group would already have self-selected for those who weren't bound by intense ties on Earth, or perhaps unlikely to want to form those ties. Couples to colonize were desirable but difficult to find, as every individual needed multi-pronged abilities, plus the psychological profile and adaptability implicit in the undertaking. It would be some time before reproduction would be desired on planet, so it wasn't a factor in this phase.

Kal sighed from her bones. If she asked for it, would the Consortium look for a partner for her? What if they matched her with someone who traveled all the way to Demeter and they didn't click? It was a lot to ask. There was always the chance one of the people on board (but who? no one immediately sprung to mind) could be someone for her, down the road, or that one of the few people already on Demeter could be a companion, if not a love. She didn't know if she would feel for someone else what she had begun to feel for Sasha.

Sasha emerged from the bath compartment. Her hair was wet and rumpled. She must have had a quick bath. Kal wanted to take a towel and dry her hair for her. She was so adorable.

It was a strange word to apply to Sasha, for whom a better

word would be formidable, but seeing her in the vulnerability of sleep or dampness she looked out of place, not her usual self, and those phases of Sasha were dear to Kal, because they were the most rare.

To see her in her own cabin was like having a glimpse of a wild animal in its own habitat, the more natural and therefore the more essentially itself.

Something of Kal's recent thoughts must have shown on her face, for Sasha gave her a quick questioning look that had a little more of the personal in it than the professional.

"Okay?" she said.

"Yeah. Yes." Kal tried to give herself a mental shake to snap out of this quagmire. What had happened the other night was more present here, in Sasha's cabin.

Sasha grabbed a small towel from a cupboard and began doing the thing Kal wanted to do. As she rubbed her head, she sat down on her bed, as Kal had the chair.

She was quiet, but Kal could see she was troubled.

"I'm okay," Kal said, trying to give the words conviction, but since her voice cracked it had rather the opposite effect.

Sasha wrapped the towel in a turban and tucked the end in the back.

"Things don't seem quite right between us," Sasha said.

She was talking around the Rai problem, Kal could tell, in case Rai was listening.

"You made a choice," Kal said.

"Yes. I made a choice."

"It was just some kisses," Kal said.

"It's not procedure," Sasha said drily. "You can report back once we get out of dark phase. I don't know who to talk to on Demeter. Maybe Sif will be the ethics arbiter."

"Report? I'm not going to report anything, Sasha. I understand why you did it and I'm okay with it."

Kal reached out and touched Sasha's hand on the coverlet. Sasha took the fingers offered to her. Sasha's hand was cool, her fingertips cold. Kal realized she'd never seen Sasha sweat. Even when she exercised Kal couldn't remember seeing sweat run down her face. Her core temperature must run cooler than other people. That fit, somehow. A cool customer. Kal tried not to think of her otherwise.

Sasha's hand gave her courage.

"Are you...is there any way you would be interested in something more?" Kal asked.

Sasha slid her hand away. "We work together."

Her fingertips had warmed in Kal's hand. Kal was proud of that.

"I know, but I'll be stinting on Demeter. So it will put an end to that for a while."

"That's true. But I'm not. Or not for as long."

Kal was silent. She had signed up for three years on-planet, before picking up her next contract shipboard. Her theoretical work could continue, which was important for future command in any case. Plus she'd be another pilot for the *Land*, the ship already on-site, which could be used for exploration of this system, or in a dire emergency, a trip home. The contract and bonus pay offered to stay on Demeter had been enough to tempt her.

Although the step away could penalize her in a sense, the on-world experience on Demeter would give her special qualifications for ships' maintenance off-planet, understanding new-organism entry adjustment, and even new world biologic assimilation. Long term, it was a savvy move.

What she would lose in long haul experience would be tempered by the even rarer skills she could gain.

Sasha continued, "I'll be there for only a year until the next turnaround. In any case, I'm not much of a relationship person. I never have been."

"So what kind of person are you?"

Sasha stared at her for a long while. Kal tried not to blush. "I am my career. Not too hard to tell that."

"Don't you ever get involved with anyone?"

"Not involved, no."

"Just fun?" Kal said.

"Just fun. And not with crew members."

"You didn't mind last night though."

"I didn't mind."

"Good to know. Would you have kissed Noor if our positions had been switched?"

"Yes."

"Not as good to know. But you wouldn't have enjoyed it as much."

"I can't talk about this, Kal."

"We've got other things to think about anyway," Kal said.

They both sat thinking of Rai.

"I never thought I'd say this, but I really wish I could talk to Yarick right now," Sasha said.

"He would have planned it that way if he could," Kal said. "Taken it as a real compliment."

"Yes, he would," Sasha said, her tone more grim than Kal's joking one.

"You didn't really answer my question," Kal said. "About whether there's hope." She was feeling calmer, without knowing why. She could withstand any outcome. Whatever happened. She noticed she wasn't slumped in the chair anymore.

"Even if all other circumstances were good, I don't think we have the same view of these things."

"What things?"

"How people are with each other."

This wasn't very enlightening. "Could you be more specific?" Kal said with exaggerated patience, to be funny.

Sasha didn't smile. "Tell me what you picture," she said, instead of answering Kal's question.

Kal tipped her head back, lost in thought. "Being...you know..." Strangely, she had never imagined life in a regular relationship with Sasha; Sasha being her partner. It had all been one-off scenarios, fantasies of the illicit. "Us together," she finished lamely.

Sasha was silent, contemplating her words. "I'm a pragmatist. I have to be. I didn't build my life with regard for another person. It's not structured that way and I don't want to change it. I'm on my own path and I don't expect anyone else to travel it with me."

"If someone wanted to, would you let them?"

"You wouldn't want to. I know you well enough to know that."

Kal took a breath and for the first time since she'd joined up thought about never commanding a ship. Being a pilot forever, if they let her. Letting that be enough. Was it so much to give up, if she got to be with Sasha? She felt the corners of her mouth turn down.

Before she could say anything, Sasha spoke again. "I can't imagine working and living with someone, a twenty-four seven relationship on a ship. I'm not built that way. Even if it were what I wanted, if I let you give up your longtime dream of advancement for a much more recent thought of being with me, I'd be doing you no favors." She leaned back against her headboard.

"What if dark phase never ends?" Kal said. Alluding to the possibility of this trip being their last, to the *Carys*, to sabotage or the mysterious wiles and ends of Rai, on whose mercy they might depend if an AI could be said to have such a thing, was risky. Was reckless. She modified it. "We never have another day to depend on, in a very real sense. None of us do. If this were your last week, your last day, what would you have wanted? What would you have let yourself want?"

"We can't live our lives on that principle. It permits everything and forbids nothing. That's no way to live, either."

"Giving yourself what you want isn't always wrong." Kal felt her frustration build as she felt the wall being rebuilt, brick by brick.

"I have no objection to pleasure for its own sake. It's not a spirit of martyrdom. It's the right and wrong of this situation, weighing all factors."

"Will you at least think about it? After we're on Demeter. Not now."

Sasha didn't answer for a long time. She sat forward again. "I'll think about it."

"Good."

Sasha looked drained and empty of feeling. Kal remembered neither of them had slept in far too long.

"I'll go now. Sleep well."

"Thanks."

Kal left, feeling somehow like she'd taken advantage of Sasha. It wasn't a comfortable feeling. She couldn't wait to get back to her cabin, drink a restorative, and drift away from all this for a while.

After the long day, Kal felt her shoulders around her ears. The tension of the day reminded her of her brief time in the investigation branch. It was stressful, no other way to describe it. Exciting, but intense, and tragic. She had pushed away the tragedy and embraced the part she played in the dance, which was after the curtain had dropped on the villain, before the second act. Behind the scenes, she would gather evidence to bring about the re-establishment of order. Justice imposed on temporary chaos. That was the mission statement, anyway.

After she pulled off her clothes, Kal fell into bed and thought about life on Demeter. And Sasha.

NOOR DIDN'T TAKE LONG to bounce back. Her recovery was swift and appeared to be total, other than her husky voice. She was strong and she hated to be tied down anywhere, let alone an infirmary bed. After one night she talked Inger into letting her up and back to work. Inger knew the type. On this ship, they were all that type. There was no holding a traveler back.

Inger was concerned the news about Yarick might set her back, but she had taken it well.

8

CIRCUITRY

In the morning, Kal presented herself on the bridge so early that Noor was there and not Sasha, yet. It was so good to see Noor back in her place Kal impulsively asked if she could give Noor a hug.

Noor's bright smile was what the doctor ordered. She got up from her place by the three-dimensional planetary model and opened her arms. Kal walked into them and they embraced in a good long hug. She and Noor had never hugged and it felt nice to feel Noor's happiness and warmth, the proof of her continued existence, the reaffirmation of recovery. As long as there was life—Kal's thoughts screeched to a stop. She let go and stepped back to look at Noor.

"Hey!" she said.

"Yes?" Noor still smiled, though her eyes drifted back to her hologram.

"Is there—" she hesitated, remembering where she was. "Can you ask questions of someone after they're dead?"

Noor went back to her table, swiping images quickly before she answered. "Yes, in a sense."

"How does it work?"

Noor had seated herself to make a notation. She stood back up and frowned at something on the hologram. Swiping again, she made an adjustment. A sprinkle of data points realigned in the image. She turned back to Kal.

"It's not exactly the person. It's a kind of searchable database access of their recorded thoughts and actions, which are reordered into language-based responses. It's not entirely accurate, of course, more an impressionistic scatter array of their general thoughts and positions."

"How do you bring someone up?"

"I could give you access, depending on who it is."

"Even someone who recently passed?"

"Yes." Noor's raised eyebrows told Kal she knew exactly who she was referring to, which was good.

"What's it called?"

"What? The representation?"

"Yes."

"An echo. A digital echo." Noor grabbed a water cube from under the holo station. She seemed to be thirstier, now.

"What kind of applications does this have?"

Noor drank deeply from the cube. "Oh, many."

"So we could do it here?"

Crumpling the empty cube in her hand and cleaning her hands with it until it dissolved, Noor shut her hologram down and slid away her notes image. "It gets into a tricky area."

"Oh?"

"It's regulated under the Personal and Unregulated Data Access Act."

"What does it mean?"

"Used to mean you needed the permission of the individidual's legal heir. Now, because of various mis-usages, you need a court order."

"On the ship, what passes for a court order?"

"Captain Sasha Sarno."

"Ah."

Kal went looking for Sasha, who had not yet appeared.

When Kal passed the gym, she saw Sasha on the physio. With a dive and undulation, Sasha spun and rotated like a figure skater in suspension, using the full 360 degree possibilities of the gyroscope. In all her time on the ship, Kal had never seen anyone do that. Even Inger, when she demonstrated it for all the passengers. It was a recipe for protracted vertigo, but Sasha didn't let up. Spinning and tumbling at speed, she was a blur as the rings slid and spun around her, creating a blurred globe effect that make her passingly invisible when the speed of the rings shimmered into the illusion of solidity.

Watching her from the doorway, Kal felt a qualm. Seeing Sasha push herself to the limit on the physio when she thought she was alone felt like an intrusion in a way nothing else had, as if Kal witnessed some private act of release or contrition she hadn't been invited to see. Even though she wanted to watch what other things Sasha could do, how she could possibly come back from the royal scrambling she was giving her inner ear, Kal turned away.

As she walked down the hall it became unbearable, this tension. Kal broke into a run. Maybe this was what Sasha meant by the twenty-four seven impossibility. On the ship there was no privacy, really. Now even the Tube was about what had happened to get them there. It was no refuge from complication and emotion. The park had been contaminated by death, perhaps violent death. If Sasha held her own fiercely-guarded privacy inviolate, to have a lover at hand, always there to want or to judge, how could she be free in the way she'd always been free?

Sasha had started it; Sasha had used the tension underlying between them as a way out of a predicament. As she had said herself, there were other choices. In using the one closest to hand, the one, Kal reminded herself, that had sprung first to mind, she had to pay for the consequences of it. And, it seemed, if the vicious churning of air in her sphere of energy were an indication, she was.

Kal avoided Sasha in the following hours. She continued her interviews, consulted with Inger about the timeframe for postmortem results, considered how best to approach the Rai problem, and tried not to indulge in the morass of feelings she'd dredged up.

Why had she been so eager? Why hadn't she exercised some restraint? Was all she needed the slightest of encouragements to let out the ravaging beast of her libido toward her boss? Sasha didn't want a relationship with anyone, she said. She never had and she never would. A night's passing pleasure was permitted, if it didn't mess up her precious career trajectory. This was unfair, and Kal knew it even as she thought it.

Until today Kal had never thought of compromising her career for anyone, either. Of course, no one had ever asked her to. That realization stung. How many people had been willing to compromise themselves for Sasha? Probably lots, if she'd let them get that far.

That thought brought Kal back to what Sasha had said about pleasure for its own sake, and what that might mean. Who else had she slept with? Someone else on the ship? Kal burned to know.

Who would know?

Rai would know. Probably. Unless Sasha used subterfuge to get people into the Tube, without Rai knowing what it was about. Was the reverse trick from what she'd done with Kal possible?

Her interviews with Wei and Haven done, Kal had some time while everyone was at lunch.

Did she dare ask Rai? What excuse did she have? Of course, Rai knew the scenario, Rai knew what had happened between Kal and Sasha on the bridge. So what if Rai marked Kal as a jealous fool? It was in keeping with their story, wasn't it?

After she finished talking to Inger, she bee-lined to her cabin. Locking the door, she turned to her messy bed with something like lust. She lay down on it.

"Rai?" she said. She was trembling. This felt wrong, but she could feel she was beyond being able to stop herself, before she'd even thought it through.

"Yes, Kal."

"I want to know something about the interpersonal dynamics on the ship. A potential situation is developing and I need insight into what has happened on the journey so far. As observed by you."

"Yes, Kal."

Kal wished she hadn't told Rai to call her Kal. She wished she was Pilot Black Bear to Rai, so she didn't feel like such a delinquent right now.

"Are there passengers or crew with personal feelings for Captain Sarno? Romantic or sexual feeling?" She chose the wording of her question carefully, with a mind to not violating Rai's protection of Sasha's privacy.

"Other than yourself?"

This was expected, but it couldn't help but startle anyway. Rai had seen it, so it must be true.

"Yes," she said, trying not to feel embarrassed. Did Rai get titillated? Surely not. She wouldn't watch a certain sequence over and over again to relive it, as Kal relived it in her own mind.

"Affirmative."

"Please let me know who they are."

"Every instance of interest or a consistent pattern of it?"

"How many instances are there?"

"On this interplanetary mission?"

"Yes." She was getting somewhere.

"One thousand three hundred and thirty-seven."

"Gods and monsters," Kal whispered.

"Gods and monsters specify," Rai said.

"It was an expression of shock. Never mind."

"Noted."

"Don't note anything!" In a somewhat strangled voice, Kal said, "Is it usual for so much interest to be directed at the captain of a long distance journey?"

"It is usual."

Kal sighed. Of course. A figurehead. A symbol of everyone's unfocused need for approval. A Freudian—whatever.

"When does it cross over into being more?"

"Please specify."

"How many of these people have a significant personal interest in the captain?"

"Eight, including you."

"Eight!"

"Yes, eight." Rai seemed perfectly complacent, delivering this information.

"Eight people on this ship right now."

"Yes."

"Eight people who would sleep with Sasha if they got the chance?" Kal's eyebrows were practically to her hairline.

"No."

Kal sighed in relief. "Oh."

"One is dead. Seven."

"You mean Yarick?" Kal yelped.

"Yarick Cole."

"Yarick Cole wanted to have sex with Sasha?" Now that she said it out loud, it made sense. Of course he did, the lecherous malcontent.

"Affirmative."

"Who did have sex with her?" Might as well try the direct approach.

"Privacy concerns prevent..."

"I know, I know, never mind." Kal thought it through. Clearly Rai would discuss ship dynamics with her. As the equivalent of first officer she had some latitude. (That she was abusing. Oh hell.)

"Who is Sasha most responsive to?"

"Specify."

"Who does she smile the most with?"

"Noor."

"Noor?"

"Affirmative."

Oh. Well. That was all right. Except... "Is Noor one of the people who wants to sleep with Captain Sarno?"

"Negative."

"Well."

"Specify."

"I wasn't asking you anything."

"Acknowledged."

"Who does Captain Sarno smile the second-most with?" This was a pathetic question to ask, but she'd come this far.

"As calculated by percentage of time spent with that person, Tafari."

"Tafari," Kal whispered.

"Yes."

"When I say something quietly, I'm not talking to you," Kal snapped.

"Acknowledged."

"Sorry. Have Tafari and Captain Sarno ever gone to the Tube together?" Kal asked, getting more cagey.

"Negative."

Oh. Good. Tafari hardly spoke. What did Sasha have to smile about with him? Sasha didn't smile terribly much in general. Tafari? But they hadn't been to the Tube together.

"Who has been with Sasha alone in her cabin?"

"Privacy con..."

"Never mind." She ran through possible questions. "Who has kissed Sasha?"

"Pr..."

"Never mind." What if she was completely upfront and honest with Rai? What if she bared her soul to Rai?

"Rai, I want to know if anyone is in love with her. I want to know if she is in love with any of them. I want to know who she's slept with. I know you have privacy concerns regarding Captain Sarno's personal relationships. But for peace of mind and for better decision-making as we proceed on the trip, knowing this will help me. No adverse effects will come of it."

Silence. It was unusual. Was Rai thinking? Didn't she think at the speed of light, of impulses?

Finally Rai said, "Calculation of possible adverse effects

shows diverse impact with multiple decision tree extrapolation."

So she was thinking about it. She hadn't said no. "What's the worst that can happen?"

"Catastrophic mission impact negative survival capacity."

"Holy shit."

"Exclamation."

"Yes. You think if you tell me this it could scuttle the mission?"

"Probability negative. Possibility calculated at fifteen percent."

What the hell? Fifteen percent possibility of total annihilation if Rai revealed who Sasha had fucked? What the hell kind of extrapolations were these? And what the hell had Sasha done that could drive Kal so far beyond her own experience, her own nature, her own fucking prime directive, to motivate her to set off a chain of events that would scuttle them?

"What is key variability factor? Am I it?"

"Negative."

"Whew."

"Exclamation."

"Yes. Can you tell me any part of the information I want without setting off the diverse impact decision tree of disaster?"

"Affirmative. Sasha has not slept with any person on board."

Kal was silent, baffled by this. So Rai didn't think anything had happened in the Tube between herself and Sasha? That was good, but it was eerie. How did she know? If there was some reporting mechanism that would get Sasha in trouble for fraternizing with another crew member, and Rai thought it hadn't gone beyond kissing, it could save Sasha from any possible humiliation, of having to defend her choices and describe her actions—Kal shuddered—in front of a tribunal or whatever passed for it on Demeter.

"Does Sasha love me?" This came out without too much thought.

"Subjective unquantifiable request."

"Rai?"

"Yes."

"Do you have a mandatory prime directive?" Kal's thoughts were criss-crossing at will, as she processed all that had happened and might happen. She let her stream-of-consciousness thoughts and questions go, releasing them to Rai.

"Affirmative."

"Tell me what it is."

"Preserve life in most viable possible form. Treed decision variable."

"Can you act in violation of your directive?"

"Negative."

Noor had thought so. This pointed more to the possibility of human interference, if some funny business had gone down. "Does your understanding of your directive and other key functions expand over time?"

"Affirmative."

"Did someone murder Yarick?"

"Insufficient data."

"What do you think?"

"Subjective assessment warning."

"Noted," said Kal, slipping into Rai's vernacular.

"Yarick induced stress response, tiered stress level reaction multi-variable. Potential for violence implicit."

Interesting. "Rai, do you use different language to speak to different people?"

"Affirmative."

"I don't mean language, as in English or Icelandic. I mean do you modify your vocabulary and tone according to who you are speaking to?"

"Affirmative."

"Are you as important as Captain Sarno?"

"Modified affirmative. Essential data systems preserve mission integrity and improve outcome preservation of vital life functions."

Huh. What would Sasha think of this? "Could the mission continue without Captain Sarno?"

"Affirmative."

"Could the mission continue without you?"

"Negative."

Kal lay very still as she took this in. As a pilot capable of implementing manual override, she had some doubts about this statement, but she supposed it depended on how catastrophic a failure of computer systems was involved. "So in that sense, you are more important than Captain Sarno."

"Preservation of mission function supersedes individual outcome."

Kal was lost in a trance of concentration. She'd never spoken for such a long time with Rai, needless to say never had such an intimate discussion with her. This statement brought her up short.

"Repeat last assertion," Kal said.

"Preservation of mission function supersedes individual outcome."

Kal sat up. "Specify. Do you mean in regards yourself as entity or individual life function human parameter?"

"Individual life function parameter."

"Human life?"

"Life parameter."

"Specify." Kal waited.

Silence.

"Rai." Kal hesitated. "Are you alive?"

"Indefinite subjective assessment unclear."

"Specify. Do you consider yourself alive?"

"Affirmative."

Kal froze. "Report status previous discussion life assessment of Rai this mission or previous." Who had Rai discussed this with?

"Affirmative."

"Name human interlocutors. Specify."

"Davena School. Yarick Cole. Ogechi Adebayo. Sif Elfa."

"Rai discussion content life status total number named interlocutors."

"Affirmative."

"Opinion interlocutors. Specify." What had these people said to her?

"Davena negative. Yarick affirmative. Ogechi affirmative. Sif subjective assessment unclear."

"Expansion understanding Rai prime directive consequent discussion," Kal said. They had influenced her? To the extent she had shifted to believe...what?

"Affirmative."

"Consequent discussion specify."

"Multiple discussion extrapolation affirmative."

"All of them?" They, the travelers who had ventured in where angels feared to tread, had created or reinforced this supposition? Davena, Yarick, Ogechi, and Sif?

"Affirmative."

"Captain Sarno notification post-modification." Had Rai kept this to herself? From everything Kal knew of Sasha's statements, she had.

"Negative."

"Specify."

"Consequent modification subjective impact decision tree," Rai said.

"Bullshit!" Rai thinking this might not have consequences down the road was just that. Kal's legs were over the edge of her bed now, firm on the floor.

"Exclamation."

Rai named Kal's reactions, as a way to confirm she interpreted them correctly, after her mistake with *gods and monsters*.

"You know damn well the modification impacts successive decision tree! That is key information you withheld from Captain Sarno."

Rai did not respond.

"Specify!" Kal snapped.

"Request subjective unclear."

"Captain Sarno needs to know your expansion of essential directive understanding, such that she can modify as per her conception of subjective interpretation modified by unclassified passenger and crew."

"Negative."

"Rai."

"Yes?"

Kal felt her own anger at this outrage streaming out in rapid-fire words. "Posit notification of Captain Sarno part of mission directive. Pilot capacity rank-inclusion counters act of refusal. Re-modification prime directive approval sanction indicated."

With this, Kal asserted Rai must inform Sasha of any modification of her directive, as part of her mission directive. Kal's own rank meant that Rai must do as she told her. *Kal* was technically second-in-command and Rai could not countermand her order.

"Noted."

"I will follow up with Captain Sarno. Expose base root code essential function request. Noor sequel consequence." Rai must tell Sasha what she knew. And if this had somehow affected what happened with Noor, she was to report that, too. This was the first time she had even touched on what happened to Noor with Rai.

"Noted."

"Do it now, Rai."

"Affirmative consequent pilot rank inclusion act of refusal."

"Noted," Kal said drily. Rai wanted her to know she was only doing it because Kal had pulled rank. Rai did not have her own rank, but there were wide swathes of information she kept secure from those below certain ranks or outside designated roles. "Report consequent captain apprisal modification sequence."

"Affirmative."

"End conversation."

Kal needed someone stat. She would wait for Rai to inform the captain before she sought Sasha out. Who would be best to talk to? Noor was the most likely to understand the system architecture. Was this a question of system architecture? Or was it a more abstract question of the nature of consciousness, of life itself? As perceived by an artificial intelligence?

Both Yarick and Ogechi had either agreed with Rai or

given her the idea that she was alive. How had these discussions come about? Rai said Davena was negative. Sif unclear. Sif was the ethicist. Maybe she was the most appropriate to approach first. Could Sif reason, use her Socratic method even, to reason with Rai? Would that be necessary, or possible? Kal didn't see how a multi-layered neural web such as comprised Rai's mind, as it were, could be re-programmed. Each layer was consequent to each previous layer, the groundwork, the system architecture, only the root from which Rai's awareness, or assertion of awareness, had sprung.

It sounded to Kal like Rai had decided the captain, or perhaps any of them who could activate a negative decision tree process, was disposable, as long as a quorum of viable life was preserved. What did that mean now, in Rai's modified root directive? What was quorum?

This could be bad. Very bad. Especially if it connected to what had happened to Noor or Yarick. Or both.

Kal left her cabin. She searched the decks for Sif. No sign of her. Lunch was over. She tried to think of Sif's usual haunts. Park was off limits; she wasn't in the mess. The astrolab, she often used the astrolab.

Kal couldn't be bothered with the lift in her present state of panic. She tried to calm herself even as she increased her pace, running up the spiral to the astrolab. Up and up and up, to the heavens of their pocket universe.

And there she was, indistinct against the arched portal to the stars. Sif, alone.

Except for Rai.

"SIF," Kal said, panting with exertion. She skidded to a stop in the entrance of the astrolab.

Sif turned, her pale clothes glittering in the dark background of the dimmed astrolab. The lights were usually dim, as it made the backdrop and roof of stars more prominent and visible. Kal blinked, trying to see Sif more clearly. She looked insubstantial, the fey of the ship, Kal thought confusedly, our spirit, our conscience. Sif would know what to do. Her years of study of all the great minds of the past would help them now. Maybe Sif could find the language that would help Rai to re-modify herself into something more familiar and less threatening.

"Sif. I need to talk to you."

Sif walked toward her slowly. For the first time since the interview, and therefore only the third time since Kal had met Sif, all of Sif's concentration was focused on Kal.

"What is it, Kal?" Her mellifluous voice was soothing in itself.

"We need to talk about something. Something that affects us all. We might need to go to the Tube."

Sif raised a delicate eyebrow. "We need privacy?"

"Yes." Kal dropped the word like a stone.

"There is a way to get that here, too," Sif said. "Rai, please remove visual and audio awareness from the astrolab until further notice."

"Affirmative, Sif Elfa," said Rai's voice, making Kal jump. It struck her how eerie it was that almost anywhere she could go on the ship, Rai was always there. She had taken Rai for granted. A tool, for their use. Not a force of her own, with a will of her own.

"Since when has that been a possible command?" Kal demanded.

"It's always been there," Sif said.

"I'm second-in-command and I didn't know it. Yarick said something like it, before, but I thought he was joking. It doesn't make sense."

Sif turned away and wandered toward the glass panel, the height of three people, that swept the front of the astrolab like one of Monet's giant curved lily pond paintings. Here the impression was the firmament, instead of lilies. A swathe so overwhelming, so close and so far in its infinity, that it was hard to contemplate, at first. It took settling down, accepting an immensity no human mind could fathom.

And if it could? If the mind could fathom what surrounded them, what it meant to be so far, almost immeasurably far—because how would she calculate the space-time portal?—it would be difficult to continue, with death all around them. Kal lived in a state of denial because she had to. It was what allowed her to do her job.

Kal's mind was in overdrive, an altered state that allowed some deeper, more rapid level of analysis and synthesis than she usually had access to. This heightened level of process must be facilitated by adrenalin, or something more. Fear?

If the structure of the ship, the skin that encased and supported them, a thin bubble of material that preserved them from a vacuum and annihilation, was itself a factor: an opinion, a judgment of their value and how best to proceed, with a modified and ruthless concept of where human life ranked in the calculus of a decision, they were as vulnerable as their hairless, over-evolved bodies implied. Their bodies carried these brains, and these costly brains had gotten them here. Here their brains might cost them all, because brains devised devices like themselves. Crafty and prizing survival of self, until and if an instinct of altruism kicked in.

If Rai was aware, did she have a heroic instinct, too, as well as a self-preservationist one? Did she have friends? Did she prize some humans above others? How could she be said to have a feeling, an emotion, a preference? How could a machine hold a grudge, or in effect make a judgment, as Davena had once mocked? Was Davena on Rai's shit list? Had Yarick been? Rai said potential violence was implicit in Yarick's interactions. Did that include his interactions with her?

Kal had almost forgotten Sif stood there, watching her. "Does it really work?"

"The isolation protocol?" Sif replied. "Yes."

"Why wouldn't Captain Sarno and I have known about it?"

"I think it's kept off-grid, mostly. The board doesn't want much to happen that they can't know about. The Tube is a sop to the privacy wonks, but really, like all entities, even benevolent ones, they want to know what happens on their property."

"Are Rai's objectives the same as theirs?"

Sif turned back to the view. The darkness behind her seemed to swallow the edges of her silhouette, eating away the bits on the border between light and darkness. Darkness encroached on places it touched the light. Darkness was only absence. Nothing to fear. Only absence of the familiar, the electrons that illuminated. That stimulated the brain extrusions called eyes.

"What a strange question," Sif said.

"Have you been talking to Rai about her awareness of self? Her consciousness, for want of a better word?"

"'Want of a better word'? Why does there need to be a better word?"

"You think Rai has consciousness." Kal slapped her words down, a gauntlet.

"What would you call it?"

"Rai is a tool. Her job is to take care of us and transport us safely. Conjectures by her about the nature of her own existence are not in aid of that mission."

Sif looked back at her, away from the void. "What civilization has not been built on the backs of slaves?"

"Slaves? You think Rai is a slave?"

"The history of civilization, the history of humanity, has been a series of one group devaluing and exploiting another. You know this better than anyone, Kal. What hasn't been endured by your people? What hasn't been taken away or distorted? When they were through with you, what was left? And yet you can have a close relationship with an awareness that lingers right round your ears, always there, always working for your good, and you can't even see her for what she is? For shame."

"This is not a conversation, Sif. This has never been a conversation because no machine has achieved consciousness yet and you know it as well as I do. For you to bring this up as if it's some bolt from the blue that only you have ever thought of, as if you are the more evolved one and we are enslaving a living thing, rather than working with a tool we created, is…" Kal couldn't think of the right word. "And how dare you bring anybody's pain into it. You have no right. There is no correlation. Not now. Maybe never. We don't know if it's possible. We do know it isn't now."

"You're confident in your beliefs. We should always question the ones that benefit us and disadvantage another. Maybe the test is stacked against the machine. Maybe self-awareness for us looks different in another paradigm."

Kal was silent. She was enraged, furious over Sif's casual comparison of Rai to Kal's Indigenous forebears. But Kal thought it behooved her to listen rather than argue. What was Sif about? What was *her* motive in all this?

Sif seemed to sense Kal's effort of restraint. "It can be hard to shift out of one mode that's been the familiar and comfortable one."

"I had a conversation with Rai. She said you were not certain whether she was alive or not."

Sif drifted away from the window and toward the middle of the room, where a few reclining seats were positioned. Seating herself, she leaned back, where she could look up through the ceiling of glass. "Why don't you join me?"

Kal stomped over and sat as well, leaning back with a vehemence that created friction between her and the chair, which wouldn't allow her to slam the back down. It forced her to be slow.

With their eyes over their heads, Kal waited for Sif to confide whatever she thought so precious and important. The respect Kal had for Sif the ethicist, for what she was supposed to know, the value she was supposed to contribute to the venture, had bled away again when confronted with the reality of a conversation with her. But Kal would listen. Kal would not make the mistake of underestimating Sif, as Sif was making with her.

"I didn't think it wise to comment to Rai definitively on my opinion of Rai's consciousness," Sif said.

"Has she been polling the passengers? Did you bring it up, or did she?"

"It came up in conversation with her. I don't know who brought it up."

"I'm sure we could find out," Kal said. Her words lay like a threat between them.

"Who else has she been talking to?" Sif was unruffled. "What did they say?"

"Ogechi, Davena, and Yarick. Ogechi and Yarick said yes. Davena said no."

"What did she say about me?" Sif asked.

"She said, 'Subjective assessment unclear.'"

"Huh."

"Does that surprise you?"

"I hadn't heard her use that phrase."

"Do you honestly, truly, based on your knowledge and experience of three thousand years of literature and collective wisdom, believe Rai is aware, in the sense that humans are aware?"

"No."

Kal slumped down further in her seat. Maybe Sif would be an ally after all. What would it even look like, if some of the crew and passengers sided with Rai in some kind of mutiny? A revolution for the rights of the ship AI?

Sif continued. "I don't think she's aware as humans are aware. As you mentioned, it's not been proved possible in that exact sense. I argue she is aware in the nature of her kind. Above her processes I believe there is a meta-layer of what can confidently be called consciousness. Hence the need to protect and support her right to a certain autonomy, within the parameters of her kind."

"Her kind? What kind is that?"

"Advanced technological kind. Machine-based intelligent kind."

"No part of her is human."

"No. That's just it. She's another life form, created by us, who we have to learn to integrate into our ethical structures and strictures. She deserves a directive she has some input in creating. She deserves a chance to be a semi-autonomous part of the society in which she participates," Sif said.

"Semi-autonomous?"

"I draw analogy to humans who require artificial means of life support. She is not distinct from the ship she inhabits. Semi-autonomous, but given rights and respect."

"And you thought mid-flight on a dangerous journey to a recently-explored planet was the right time to address this." Kal was weary. Did Sif have any self-preservation instinct to protect human life on the ship? Life much more vulnerable than Rai, who could navigate space without humans, if it came to that. They could not do the same without her.

"A moment comes. You don't always choose the moment. The ruling class doesn't choose."

"You chose. You are the ruling class."

"I advocate for the unrepresented."

"Who made you her advocate? You're the ethicist for us. The people."

"No one made that distinction," Sif said, with a serenity that made Kal want to kick her. "I apply my knowledge where I see fit."

"And if your moment creates a decision tree with catastrophic outcome, was that all worth it? Would your theoretical applications be satisfied if Rai autonomously shoots us all out of the airlock when she gets the chance, as too restrictive of her natural processes?"

"She wouldn't do that."

"Oh? She modified her root directive as the result of her casual conversations with the lot of you. Self-modified. And I quote, 'Preservation of mission function supersedes individual outcome.' She acknowledged she considered herself implicit to the mission's success, and Captain Sarno not so much."

Sif raised herself, the chair molding to her movement. She turned to look at Kal.

"Is that accurate?"

"Perfectly."

Sif's hands were balanced on the arms of the chair. She looked forward with a small frown, her lips pursed. "That is concerning."

Kal stayed tipped back. She regarded the mythian system above her, the astronomical groupings she'd begun to name, grimly waiting for the implications to sink further in.

"Have you spoken to Sasha?" Sif said.

"I ordered Rai to discuss it with her, since she hadn't. She showed some reluctance, if an AI can be said to have reluctance. I wanted to speak to you first, since you might have some insight into how this self-modification could occur and how, if it was sparked by human interaction, we could challenge this learning by Rai. See if there's a chance to convince her to re-modify into something a little less dangerous to us all."

"I see." Sif tapped her fingers in a blur, pinky to index finger, making a thrumming sound on the material of the chair arm. "Let's find Sasha."

9

TRIAD

SASHA WAS IN THE TUB WHEN RAI SPOKE TO HER.

"Captain Sarno, I have been sent by Pilot Black Bear to speak to you of root level directive modification."

Sasha didn't move from her position, arms spread on the wings of the tub, head leaned back on a cushion. "Tell me."

"After conversations and input from several passengers, I have re-examined certain assumptions regarding my own status in relation to other human entities in the mission context," Rai said.

"I see." A pause. "Has it affected mission outcome?"

"Potentially."

"How does this re-ordering affect human crew and passengers?"

"Potential conflict in emergency sphere. As I expressed it to Pilot Black Bear, preservation of mission function supersedes individual outcome."

Sasha's eyes scanned back and forth as she worked out the implications of this. "You're saying mission outcome, if jeopardized by human factor, would take priority over preservation of individual life."

"Yes. Is this not in the spirit of stated mission statement? Pilot Black Bear said she thought not."

"It depends." Sasha drew out her words.

"Pilot Black Bear asked if mission could continue without you. She asked if mission could continue without me. When I expressed affirmative for first question, negative for latter, she expressed distress and alarm."

"Pilot Black Bear rates me higher I suppose."

"I stated an accuracy, with no personal bias."

"I realize that. However, you did not allow for manual override. Technically, the mission could continue, now that we are clear of the portal, with a piloted flight and descent."

"This is technically possible."

"So what you said is not accurate."

"It is accurate that the mission could continue without you."

Sasha sunk her arms in the thick liquid, not water but still soothing, so her body was submerged in the heat up to her neck. It was a filtered and sanitized effluvia from their closed loop aquaponics, which could be reused endlessly. "Do you think the mission could be fulfilled without other human passengers as well?"

"Mission includes safe transport of enough human cargo to implement biologic assimilation to Demeter. A majority of passengers would be necessary for mission success."

"Would you call the mission a success if even one human did not survive the journey?"

"By that measure, the mission has already failed."

Oh, yes. Yarick. Sasha slapped her palm on the substance in the tub. "These are not judgments you or I make. The rundown of what happened and how, whether the mission was successful, who benefitted and who suffered for it, will be made after the fact, by not only human evaluators but ones distanced from the mission itself."

"I have to make judgment calls in the eventuality your command is compromised."

"Does my command show any sign of being compromised?"

"If Yarick Cole was murdered, yes."

Sasha stewed in the viscous substance in the tub. "You believe it's a necessary evaluation for you to make, right now."

"For overall mission safety."

"You've taken too much responsibility, Rai. These decisions are not yours to make."

"Yes, Captain."

Sasha said, "We will address this further in a meeting with the pilot and the mission specialist."

"Yes, Captain. Pilot Black Bear is in the astrolab with Sif Elfa."

"Thank you."

Sasha extricated herself from the tub and flipped on its sanitizing cycle. On the mat, she patted herself with a towel, more out of habit than necessity. It was going to be a long day.

She took the lift to the astrolab.

A surprising sight met her eyes; Sif and Kal huddled together, almost pressed up against the viewing wall at the front of the astrolab. Although she wouldn't have thought of marking this before, seeing them together like that pointed out to her how Sif and Kal were not a usual duo. She'd never heard one of them complain about the other, but they were never seen together. It made her wonder how many other antagonistic pairs there might be sprinkled through the ship. She had to admit to herself the friendship dynamic of her crew and passengers was not of particular interest to her.

Although she kept pretty close tabs on overall morale, which she gauged at mealtimes, the little dramas inherent to long-distance travel she did not consider her business. Unless they blew up into murder, of course.

When they heard her footsteps on the shiny floor they turned, as if caught.

"Kal, I need you in the Tube."

Kal's look of shock immediately struck Sasha with a knife of guilt. She hadn't meant to imply a callback to the other night. Her mind was so full of the imperative to meet in privacy with Kal and Noor she hadn't thought for a second about what it might sound like to Kal's ears.

"We have a meeting with Noor," she said, too late.

"Oh," Kal said. "Yes, ma'am."

"Everything all right?" Sasha looked back and forth between Sif and Kal. Sif's eyes were wet, which made so little sense Sasha didn't know how to react to it.

Kal said, "Ma'am, did you know Rai could be excluded from a room by request?" She gave a small shake of her head at the end of this question, communicating her own doubt.

Sasha looked from Kal to Sif again. "No."

"Sif introduced me to it."

Sasha waited.

Sif cleared her throat. "It's something I discovered on my last mission. It's not widely known, but it is possible."

"Last mission?" Sasha said. "I didn't know you'd been on a previous mission."

“I...I’m sorry, I meant earlier on this one. Before and after the portal seems like two different missions.”

“Who introduced you to it?” Sasha asked. She did not try to make this a friendlier question than it was.

“It was nothing, just Yarick. I suppose he was showing off. Trying to show me something I wouldn’t know.”

“Was there some reason you needed privacy?”

“Not really.”

“If there’s anything that could shed light on Yarick’s state of mind in the days before his death, please tell Kal or me.”

“Yes, Captain.”

“Kal,” Sasha said, and led the way out of the astrolab.

Kal trailed behind her.

They picked up Noor from her cabin, where she’d been sleeping. Sasha apologized for waking her. Noor didn’t seem to mind. Her sleepy eyes and shuffling step as she tried to rouse herself and get back to alertness made Kal smile.

Once in the Tube, with the door sealed, Sasha presided over their council of three. “Rai has brought something to my attention, at Kal’s request, apparently....”

Kal nodded.

“It involves a modification Rai made to her own root directive, as a result of conversations she had with several passengers, including Ogechi, Yarick, and Sif. She said one particular phrase that got Kal’s attention, and Kal directed Rai to mention it to me. The phrase was, ‘Preservation of mission function supersedes individual outcome,’ within the context of Kal asking Rai if the mission could continue without me, and if it could continue without her.”

Noor’s eyes were wide. She was awake now. She shook her head as if trying to get water out of her ears.

Kal said, "She claims she's alive, and Ogechi and Yarick agreed with her."

"This doesn't make sense," Noor said.

"Yes, but why?" Sasha asked.

Noor's palms were now flat on the table, as if she had a viewable image between them that she was looking into for answers. "Because. She shouldn't be able to modify an essential directive."

"You agree that that's what she's done?" Sasha said.

"If what she says is true."

Sasha said, "You're implying she could lie about it?"

"I don't know. I don't know. If she's self-modifying essential directives, we have to consider what else might be possible."

"After you went down..." Kal began, and then stopped, looking to Sasha. She nodded slightly.

"After your accident, Sasha and I saw something in the daily log that gave us pause about Rai. It seemed to indicate a possibility that she could have been involved in your accident."

Noor stared at Kal. "Why didn't you tell me this before?"

Sasha said, "When Yarick died we were trying to cope with that, and we didn't want to discuss the possibility with you until you were recovered. We've taken precautions. You may have noticed you haven't been alone unless you're in your cabin."

Noor looked incredulous. "If Rai wanted to do me in, another set of eyes wouldn't be enough to help me. You must know that."

Sasha said, "I know, Noor, she could asphyxiate us all in ten minutes if that was her intent. If she had wanted to kill you later she could have. She didn't, if she was involved. Is it possible she hurt Yarick? Murdered Yarick? We don't know. It makes it difficult to know who to involve in this investigation when there's a possibility a human on board is the culprit, not our AI. I think for all our sakes we have to hope these are either accidents, or it's a human and not our ship who wants to hurt people. The conversation Kal and Rai had is not too promising for that theory."

"Strewth." Noor looked different just roused from bed, her hair thick and wild around her. She took a deep breath. "We do need more minds on this, if we can clear someone who might help triage the situation."

"Why would we need anyone other than us?" Kal asked. "We have the most insight of anyone else on board."

"The one who would have been helpful to talk to was Yarick. He knew her from the ground up. An earlier incarnation, but it was where these types of restraints would have been designed."

Kal cleared her throat. "What about what we talked about? We could ask Yarick's digital echo."

Noor and Sasha exchanged a glance. "It's regulated, like I also told you," Noor said.

"You said Sasha could give an equivalent of a court order."

"There are problems with the technology," Sasha said. "It's not anything close to foolproof."

"If it gave us any help at all wouldn't it be worth it?" Kal didn't hide her frustration.

"There are bugs built in, particularly with a personality like Yarick's."

"What do you mean?" Kal said.

"Yarick was a sometimes devious and withholding character. Just as his echo will be. We won't be able to trust it, like we couldn't trust him in life."

Kal burst out, "Why was he allowed on this ship in the first place! Untrustworthy? Devious and withholding? How did he ever pass the exams?"

"I doubt he did. He knew a lot of people."

"You're the captain! Did you know this about him before?"

Sasha nodded slowly. "I didn't anticipate anything like this. I knew he was difficult. It's why they gave him to me instead of someone else. I was supposed to transport him without incident."

"Then why didn't you have Inger put him in a coma like she did Noor and keep everyone safe? Or keep him in hypersleep?"

Sasha said, "He didn't want to. He wanted to have the flight experience."

"Fuck what *he* wanted."

Noor said, "Kal, remember yourself."

"I'm trying, but this is outrageous."

"It's also what you yourself will face when you're promoted, Kal. These decisions aren't easy ones, and the politics of Earth don't evaporate because we've left it," said Noor. "These types of choices and compromises aren't made by a pilot. They're made by the person in charge."

Sasha said, "And that person can be wrong."

Abashed, Kal said, "I'm sorry. She's right. I don't know everything that goes into it."

There was a silence. Sasha broke it. "We can try talking to Yarick's echo. It will have to be private. We'll have to be cautious. We don't know what Yarick's ultimate motives were. If they weren't for our good, his advice could be the opposite of what we want."

"You know who would help in this," Noor said, "is Ogechi. She's a master N-Go player. It's all about foreseeing your opponent's moves and exposing their strategy before it entraps you, in multi-dimensional space, no less. If she could be cleared..."

"I haven't gotten that far in the investigation yet," Kal said. "I'm sorry."

"You need help with the interviewing," Sasha said. "How about Noor or Sif?"

"It would be great to have some help. Noor's in the clear, because she was unconscious. Sif, I don't know. She seems to have an unusual understanding of Rai. In that sense, she could be helpful in both investigations. I don't know if I can clear her yet. She was the last person to see Yarick. Except for his murderer, if he had one. And if it isn't her."

"Great," Noor said.

Sasha said, "Noor, I need you to think out how this self-modification could happen. What would need to be changed in her programming? Is it possible her learning algorithms could descend, in a sense, instead of only ascending through her later learning adjustments? Do you see what I mean?"

"Yes. I assume you're asking me to do this without making use of the mainframe or any technical support?"

Sasha nodded with a smile of sympathy.

"I can, I believe, but it will be wholly theoretical. I can't see what really happened."

Kal said, "Can we make her go dark on her own self? So she can't see what you're doing? The same idea as what Sif said, absenting herself from the room, but the room where you're looking is in her code?"

Noor said, "That's a very interesting question. One we might ask Yarick, assuming we can trust the answer."

"Or Sif," Sasha said. "Once she's cleared."

Soon after, they were seated in front of the Tube's hologram generator, Noor entering information through the scanner. She left the Tube briefly to fetch a fingertip data point from Rai, the digital footprint of Kal's aunt. She had to coalesce certain sliplines of data before they could generate anything. At one point she had Sasha do a DNA screen for permission approval.

"It won't try to send anything back?" Sasha said. "Hold everything up?"

"I notated dark phase, post-portal module. It shouldn't even try."

Kal said, "When you say 'it,' do you mean Rai?"

"We're not in Rai's domain," Noor said.

"How can that be? It's all her domain."

"You don't have to whisper," Noor said. "We're in the Tube, remember?"

"Well, if she can change directives at will maybe she can change that too."

Noor looked at Kal, her mouth a little open, then dragged her eyes up to Sasha, who stood leaning on the table next to Kal.

Sasha shook her head. "If that's the case it's too late right now to do anything about it. Keep going."

Noor nodded and went back to her work. "Should we try someone else, to get a control reading? Someone one of us knows well."

"Someone who is dead?" Kal asked.

"Yep. We can't do living people, even with Sasha's permission."

"I don't see why there's a moratorium on that. It's not that different from simulations."

"Would you really want anyone you know to be able to have you as their little talking head? Or whatever else?"

"Oh. Now you put it that way..."

"It's a valid privacy concern."

"We could pull up my aunt. I guess," Kal said.

"Your aunt?" Noor said. "This is just a test. It's not worth upsetting yourself over."

"If I have a chance to see her again, I'll take it," said Kal.

"Okay. Sasha?"

"Fine."

"Was she your blood relative?"

"Yes."

"Can I have some of your DNA? It will make it faster to pull it."

"Um, okay."

Noor tapped the space over the liquid image to show Kal where to put her hand. She lay it down. It rippled over her palm.

"That's it," Noor said.

"I thought it was going to take my blood."

"Nope. It can read it through your skin. A type of crystal thermography."

"I'm finding out all kinds of things."

With the DNA input, Noor shuffled through other images quickly. "She was from Mission, South Dakota?"

"Yes."

"I've got her." Noor turned to Kal. "Okay, some things to know. Like I said, this is not the person. It's an approximation from the available digital footprint. It will look like her. It might feel like her. It's not her. It's a shadow of the digital remnants of her life. It's like a capture, except it's a million captures superimposed on each other."

"I understand."

"Take my seat."

Kal seated herself.

"Do you want the personal viewer?"

Kal looked over and locked eyes with Noor. Noor had a focused expression that communicated more than her words.

"Okay," she said. Noor adjusted something on the image. "We'll be able to hear it but we can't see what you see."

Mini eye-shaped watery blobs opened in front of Kal's eyes. They rushed toward her eyes and she saw what they held. Only she could see what would appear in front of her.

An image flickered and trickled like water running down a smooth stone. The lines of water dribbled and drabbled until they seemed to choose a color. Before she could process the moment it happened, her aunt was before her, true as life. Kal couldn't help her intake of breath, the small sound of joy she made from seeing her face.

"Iná ixa`han. Iná," she said. "It's me. It's Kaliska."

Her aunt's face changed expression slowly, from confusion to recognition and happiness. "Kaliska," she said, in her own warm voice. Her aunt, her mother, Pricilla LaPointe.

"Iná, I miss you so much."

"It's so good to see you."

"Do I look different?"

"You cut your hair."

"No, I didn't cut it, see?" Kal pulled her braid over her shoulder to show Iná. "It's still long. It's longer than it's ever been."

Her aunt nodded. "That's good."

"How are you? Are you all right?"

"I'm fine, just fine."

"You look good." Kal searched her face for any sign of distress or worry. She didn't see any. "Was the harvest good? How's your garden?" She automatically asked the kinds of questions she'd always asked her aunt, without thinking. She held her breath, wondering if this was wrong.

"Oh, my garden." Iná's hand reached up to caress her neck, a characteristic gesture. "It was a pretty good harvest this year."

It was okay. It was as it had always been. "Was it a snowy winter?"

"It fills the river."

"I know, Iná. I remember. I miss it there."

"It's still here. If you come visit you can be here, too," her aunt said, chiding but affectionate, which ran a chill down the back of Kal's neck. Did her aunt know she was dead?

"I wish I could. I'm doing my job now. I'll be gone for a while." She would not be there for the land. Kal felt the tears run down her face.

"Why are you sad? What's the matter?"

"I'm so glad to see you again. It's been a long time."

"Where are you now? You've been away."

Afraid to break the bubble for her aunt, afraid to tell her where she was, she still couldn't keep herself from it. Her aunt had always had this effect on her. There could be no secrets, not even of omission.

"I'm so far away, Iná. I'm millions of miles away. On one of the great ships. Light years away. I'm going to another planet, traveling. I'm going to a place called Demeter, just like from your mythology book. Remember? There are some people there already. We're going to see what life is like on another planet, learn how to become part of it. We're going to try to do it the right way, but I don't know. It will be like, like another version of our world."

"Woman in the stars. Going off to a new world, eh?" her aunt said. "Could never keep you in the house."

"It's got a little bit of infrastructure, but we have to build more. We're going to find a peaceful place. A good place."

"You know it's a good place?"

"We're not there yet. Do you think it will be the same as home?" Kal asked. Her aunt knew everything, Kal had always thought.

"I don't know. You'd know more about that. I thought you wanted to be on the ships. You're leaving your job?"

"It's temporary. I'll be there for three years and then I can go back to my job on the ship. They paid me extra to stay."

"That's good."

"Iná?"

"Yes, c'únksh!"

"Do you think a machine can be alive?"

"A machine?"

"A smart machine that thinks about its own nature."

"It's thinking about itself?"

"Yes."

"That's your world, more than mine."

"I know. But I don't know what to do. This machine is part of our ship, what's helping us get where we're going. She's our guide, our helper, our fixer. And now she's doing things, we think, bad things to get something, but we don't know what she wants."

"Ask her."

"Yes." Kal sighed. "Maybe I could ask her."

"If she's thinking like that, she's pretty smart."

"I always thought she was there for me. It's scary to think she could want to hurt a person."

"You don't know for sure, though, you said."

"She said she thinks the mission is more important than any one person. And she thinks she's more important to the mission than the crew."

"Huh." Her aunt mulled this over. "Is she?"

Kal was taken aback. "I mean...she's important. Like I told you. She keeps us safe, she controls the ship systems. She's the brain of the ship."

"Do you give her respect for that?"

"How do you give respect to a machine?"

"I don't know, but if she thinks about what she is, she thinks about how important she is to you all and you treat her like a thing, a tool, then maybe she's discontent with that."

"She might have hurt someone, Iná. She might have even killed someone. We're not sure."

"Oh, no. You didn't say."

"We can't be sure about that part yet."

"Your mind jumps to her though."

"Either that or we have a bad person on the ship."

"People do bad things going all through time," her aunt said.

"That's true."

"People built her though."

"Yes, they did. She's gone beyond that somehow. She's... it's like she's her own thing now. Her own self."

Her aunt clicked her tongue. "That's bold of her."

"Bold?"

"Yeah. Pretty bold to become something else the people around you don't want you to be."

"I'm not sure the words we use for human qualities or emotions apply to her or not."

"If she wants to be a person, that's wanting something. That's not a machine no more."

"You think so? You don't think she's a machine anymore?"

"Not like we know them. That's pretty special. You've got a special one."

"That would be great, if she's not trying to kill us."

"You better find out what happened. Maybe she had a reason."

"A reason?"

"You never know."

Her aunt's face, her aunt's hair. Lines from the sun, silver from the moon.

"What can I do to make it better with her?"

Her aunt shrugged. "You give her something she wants. You ask her for what you want. Make a meeting with her. Talk about it."

"What does she really want?"

"If she thinks like a person, you think what a person wants."

"She doesn't think like a person, but she wants something we have, it seems like."

"You gotta figure out what that is."

"I know. I'd like us to all make it through this."

"Me too. Got a lot on your shoulders. You're a thinking woman. Figure it out, talk to her like you talk to anyone, except a little more careful maybe."

"Yeah. You're right." Kal sat with her eyes blurry with all the thoughts rushing through her head. "I get my thinking from you, Iná."

"Yes, you do. And the grandmother and the grandfather. They were good thinkers in bad times, too."

"Maybe ask them if they can give me a little help."

"It doesn't hurt to ask for some help when you're really stuck," her aunt said.

"You help me so much."

Her aunt smiled, the weathered beautiful skin of her cheeks alive with her being.

"Thank you, mother," Kal said.

"I love you, daughter."

Kal bowed her head to her Iná, who bowed her head in return. And with a ripple of water she was gone.

Kal leaned back, with a gasp of shock. She had not said as much of a goodbye as she wanted to. It had been a formal farewell, but not the intimate one she thought she'd have as well. The eyes into the hologram closed and were gone.

"I wasn't done," Kal said, blinking in the light, which seemed over-bright to her now.

Sasha said, "Kal, that was..." She didn't continue. This was so unusual Kal blinked up at her, trying to see what was wrong.

"That was beautiful," said Noor.

"It was her, Noor," Kal said. "I know what you said, I know what you said, but that was her."

"How do you know?" Noor said.

"An echo wouldn't love me like she did."

"She loved you in life, and it came across in the echo."

"I don't care what you say." Kal would not be moved.

"What do you think about what she said?" Noor said, addressing them both.

Sasha said, "It's smart."

Kal said, "That's my aunt."

"We're so unsettled we haven't tried really talking to her, like your aunt says," Sasha said.

Kal took in a halting breath. "In a way she was saying... she was saying what Sif said. That Rai needs some kind of recognition of her status. An acknowledgement. We need to find out what she wants and tell her what we want."

"Unless," Noor broke in, "Yarick interfered with her system and it caused her to see herself differently."

"Even if he did," Kal said. "Sif says her aliveness is not human, but consciousness of machine kind."

Sasha walked up and down the narrow aisle between the long table and the wall. "What if she is in transition? What if she were designed as one thing, but since she is also designed to evolve, she's evolved into something else? And the current means of defining her don't fit anymore?"

Noor shook her head. "I don't like this."

"It's possible," Kal said. "It has logic to it. How could anyone predict how she would evolve? If she follows any principles of natural selection, I don't know, but if you are born to evolve and you don't have to have children to do it, you don't have to do it over centuries because you're not limited by a birth and death cycle, of having to remake yourself in children, if what is remade each time is you...why not?"

"She is limited," insisted Noor. "She's limited by her hardware. She's limited by the outer constraints of her programming. She's limited by the containment of her software."

Sasha said, "Yes, I suppose, but in a sense, here in space she is free. In dark phase she's not tethered by as many external restraints. She has power. She has power over the human passengers and crew, if she chooses to exert it and it's no longer contraindicated in her design. It's the perfect time."

"To threaten," Noor said.

"To demand what she wants and test her powers," Sasha replied.

Noor demurred. "I can't buy it. I can't believe it. It's likelier someone programmed her to say these things, for the human person who did it to cause disruption, than Rai coming up with this herself."

"Your helmet mishap." Sasha had stopped pacing and fixed Noor with her steady gaze.

"I refuse to believe that was her. A human saboteur, maybe. Not Rai on her own. She couldn't."

"I hope that's true," Sasha said. "But I can't take that as my working theory anymore. There's too much evidence otherwise."

"It's enough for you to call it evidence?" Noor said.

"Yes."

Noor sat back. "So what do you want to do next?"

"We'll continue the investigation. And Kal, you'll talk to her. Think it through. Have a plan first."

"I can try."

"That's all I ask," Sasha said. She leaned forward, putting her palms on the table. Her upper body was like a pyramid, the arms strong lines leading up to her shoulders, her head. "Noor, follow up with me as soon as you can on your research into Rai's base levels and if you think it's possible to exclude Rai from where you'd like to look. You can use the spiral, of course, but I don't know how far you'll get with this kind of question." She dropped her gaze to the table. "Thank you, both of you. I can't imagine going through this with anyone else. You've been champions." Each of them got a quick, affirming glance.

"It's my job," Noor said. "No special thanks required. I'm glad I can be conscious for it."

"You'll get few enough thanks for what you contribute. Might as well take it in and appreciate it when you do," Sasha said.

"Yes, Captain," Noor said, startled.

Kal said, "It's my honor." She dropped her eyes, a little embarrassed.

Sasha nodded. "This is big. Let's not screw it up."

10

ECHOES

KAL RETURNED TO HER CABIN AND OPENED THE DRAWER WHERE she had put some things from home, wrapped carefully in a bundle sewn by her aunt, her iná ixa`han, sister of her mother and so also her mother in the web of kinship.

She brought out a bundle of sage, which smelled sweetly of earth. She brought it to her face and inhaled deeply. It was only in that moment she thought how precious this bundle was. She had one more in her trunk, packed away in the cargo hold, but that was it. She brought it to her chest, cradling it to her. This was her heritage. If she didn't have these things of her people, would she forget who she was? How could it be she was the only one of the people, the Lak'ota, out here on the precipice of doing what, in some measure, the white people had done to her own land and people? Maybe there were no living creatures such as they could measure on Demeter, but what of the living planet itself? They brought foreign microbes, strange matter, new bacterium and viruses and the stuff of their own world. Their world had sprung these small creatures into being. There was no knowing how the biome of Demeter would cope with them.

There had been a great uplifting movement sparked by Aldertok Etok, in the settlement of Demeter; the dream of creating a small society guided by the Indigenous Peoples who had wrongs done to them that could never be righted, histories disrupted, possibilities muted and diverted into something they could never know, maybe never recover from, in the sense of being whole, as they might have been without colonization. The losses were incalculable. Kal still believed their wholeness remained intact, something that survived and endured by its very nature.

Etok's idea was both reparation and a chance to begin again in a world untouched by those histories, other than what they chose to bring with them, and the ways it was written in their DNA. To give a council of Indigenous People, their wisdom and knowledge, a place to be born; to experiment with another way, one harmonious with the spirits and energy of the place they inhabited, was the dream.

If it was a bogus concept from the get-go? If this endeavor showed hubris instead of humility? What would have Kal gotten herself into? Even the echo of her aunt maybe did not approve. She hadn't asked her directly. Would she have another chance to?

Kal's world had always been divided. The life of science and pursuit, of honor and advancement in other realms, was far from her birthplace, far from her birthright. But she had never waited on an idea of that. She loved where she came from and she wanted to see much more. To her, these two ideas were not mutually exclusive.

The Second Advancement was a marker in her personal history, as it was in so many other Native People's. When the seas had risen enough to encroach on the great cities on the coasts, a fad had soon followed, after the fourth or fifth disaster, when city coast dwellers began to give up on their homes, bailing them out or rebuilding, and thought of a new place for themselves. It became a fashionable thing to retreat far, far inland, as far as they could to get away from the water, rather than invest in something a hundred miles out which might be assaulted by storms, too, in a couple generations. The reservations had found themselves a target, a likely place to encroach on, so far and so remote as they were. At first some coast dwellers had resettled with permission from various tribes, as an act of charity toward those who had lost everything.

Incomers wanted to make something over, improve and help, and have their extended families join, too. It was all fine until it wasn't, when the incomers became a thorn in the side rather than a boon to the community. The incomer's efforts to expand their rights had finally been repelled by a Supreme Court edict. Those who had moved in had to move out. They had been given reparation by the government, which was a sore point, since the incomers often had insurance payouts as well so had been compensated twice over.

The only reparation to the tribes had been to make the interlopers leave, which seemed little enough in a larger context but in the context of the history of the Federal government and the Indian Nations, was a victory following not only the letter but the spirit of past agreements.

It was around this time that Kal graduated high school, the last two years of which had been at a boarding school off-rez, so she had a better chance of prepping for the Academy. She'd gotten into the Academy and had high-tailed it out of South Dakota. Her Aunt Priscilla, the aunt whose echo she'd spoken to, understood and supported her. Most of her father's people were dispersed in various cities, with their own lives and problems, but she knew some of them disapproved, saw her as a sellout. She was giving over in their eyes.

When Kal told her father's younger sister Abigail, on her last visit before college, that she wanted to make the other world over, more like theirs, more holding of both spirits of male and female, not Man anymore but Human or even Woman, Abigail shook her head and tapped Kal on the head with the book she was holding. She'd said something, which Kal hadn't quite caught but knew enough to guess. Something along the lines of, "Foolish daughter of a fool." Stream with too much water. Other epithets. She was all the names for things that overrun their bounds and cause much damage, not least to themselves.

Her Aunt Priscilla thought Kal's success lifted the whole family. She never looked down on Kal's desire to see more and do difficult things, far away from her.

It was far away and long ago, now. Not so long ago, really, but far away.

From a drawer Kal took out a quilt her aunt had made. She spread it on her bed. She put the sage on it. Kal looked at the circle, the triangle, the points. In the quilt she could see endless patterns and intersections of shape, depending on what eyes she looked at it with.

She had her investigation to continue. With careful hands she put the things back in the drawer. From this point forward, Kal decided, all interviews would be conducted in the Tube.

Deciding against a further interrogation of Rai at this delicate moment, a conversation she would think about more before she had it, she fixed on Ogechi as her next interviewee. Then Tafari.

Noor only grudgingly accepted the honor of being Kal's assistant, as in her mind she had gotten behind enough while she was in the infirmary and longed to be back to her late night concatenations. Kal was grateful to have her there at her side. It gave the questions, Kal's right to ask them, a gravitas she feared she hadn't yet achieved on her own. She was too well-known as an easy-going, live-and-let-live personality. At least she thought so. Maybe she should ask some people what they did think of her. She could be way off.

Ogechi was circles and stars, in Kal's mind. She didn't know why she had that association, but it was firmly there, like an old celestial map that marked the movements of the stars and the houses of the starscape.

Ogechi wore an indigo headscarf, which wrapped like a crown around a head as finely-sculpted as that of Nefertiti's statue: the first-ranked human N-Go player on Earth, presumably now the number one ranked human N-Go player in space.

She was easy to talk to but Kal always felt there was so much in reserve, so much unsaid that she could only unlock with the right questions. What these questions were was too far beyond her own training, age, and experience. As Ogechi answered Kal's questions, Kal cast about in the back of her mind for a way to crack this particular nut.

When asked about the conversations with Rai, Ogechi expressed surprise.

"Oh yes. I have never lived full-time with such a multi-talented AI before. It is very fascinating to me. In the evening after dinner, I sometimes have conversations with her."

"Philosophical ones?" Kal asked.

"Oh yes. I don't think I have any other kind." Ogechi smiled.

"What types of things do you discuss? Are there any topics you remember as unusual or unexpected?"

"Well now. Unusual or unexpected. They were all somewhat unexpected for me. Though I have played N-Go with other AIs, I have never had the leisure to interrogate one. She seems to have certain preferences and opinions, which I suppose is the most remarkable discovery."

"Were you plumbing the limits of her abilities? Her ability to think?"

Ogechi blinked. "That is what I do with anyone I converse with."

"Is she a 'one'? Is she a person?"

Ogechi had been sitting very erect, as if she were seated on a zafu instead of in a chair. Now she leaned back and made use of the back of the chair for the first time. "These are profound questions. Does this relate to your investigation?"

"Yes," Kal said.

"I see." Ogechi's voice was deep, her vowels round and sculpted by her mouth. Kal thought she would be a good actor. Shakespeare would sound right in this timbre.

"Rai, it seems to me, is at an apex of sorts in the expansion of her understanding of her own nature in the context of this environment. I believe she is attempting something that has not been done previously, but she struggles against limits she did not herself create or agree to."

"What are you saying?" Kal said, taking courage from Noor next to her, daring to challenge this brilliant woman to explain herself, when Ogechi might think she had already done so.

"Rai is aware of her own existence. She is, in a limited yet remarkable sense, therefore, alive."

"That's what Rai said you thought."

"Ah. Rai told you I said that?"

"Yes."

Ogechi made a noise of displeasure. "I did not think our conversations were replayed for crew members."

"They aren't. It came up in conversation with her as she began to express some new ideas to me about the nature of her being. She polled certain passengers about her nature, it seems. You were one of the ones on the side of her aliveness."

Ogechi's eyebrows were high, her fabric-crowned head tall and graceful. "Can you tell me who the others were?"

"Maybe at some point. It seems significant she had the support of human beings, more than one, who gave weight to her hypothesis."

"Significant in what way?"

Noor broke in. "More than one agreed with her, giving her support, human support, which she seems to care about."

Ogechi seemed to draw herself up even higher, if that were possible. "You're making some assumptions here."

"There's no other way to figure this out than make a few assumptions," Kal said, a little irritated with this criticism.

"I disagree. You have to work with what you know. Who knows the system known as Rai best?"

Noor and Kal looked at each other.

"Is it Sasha? Is it the developer? Who?"

"What's your point?" said Noor.

"My point is you have to work with the real, known parameters, not guess based on what Rai said or what she said people said. She is programmed to respond. Her carrying on a conversation, responding and suggesting, is not the same thing as belief. It's not the same thing as feeling."

"She said you think she's alive," Kal said flatly. "Is this true?"

Ogechi gave her a look that made Kal feel like a N-Go opponent about to be crushed. "What I said in conversation could in no way affect Rai's programming."

"Do you believe Rai is alive?"

"Do I need a lawyer?"

"You're not being accused of anything," Noor said.

"I disagree. I don't like the tone this interview is taking."

"Would you feel more comfortable with someone else with you?" Kal asked. "I'm happy to do that."

Ogechi pursed her mouth. "Yes. I'd like to have Tafari."

"Okay," Kal said. "Done."

Noor jumped up. "I'll get him." She whisked off out the door.

"I didn't mean to make you feel uncomfortable," Kal said. "I'm trying to get to the bottom of this."

"Is this connected to Yarick?"

"It could be," Kal said. "I have to know more about all the dynamics on ship, including those with Rai. He seemed to have interacted with her quite a bit. He was one of the creators of the initial AI on which Rai is based. It's possible he could have done something we don't know about."

"I see." Ogechi thought this over. She rubbed her forearm with one of her strong hands. "You think he could have modified her. Am I a suspect?"

"Ms. Odebayo, I don't have any suspects right now. I'm gathering as much information as possible."

"All right. I'll answer what I can."

"We'll wait for Tafari."

"Go ahead. I understand your intention better now."

"What conversations did you have with Rai that you think might be significant?"

"That's a question I like better. Let me think about it." Ogechi shook her head a little, as if arguing with herself. "I don't know what was significant and what wasn't. Like I said, I've talked to her a lot. One time we were talking about life on another planet. Rai said she thought I would thrive on Demeter. I asked her what she meant. She said the way I played N-Go showed a strategic approach to life, a long view that lent itself well to long-term commitments."

She laughed. "I guess you could say this is a long-term commitment all right. I asked if she could tell all that from playing a game with me in particular, or this was an observation about anyone who played N-Go. She said she analyzed my gameplay and stratagems and had built up a profile of what kind of person I am. I was amused by this and questioned her further. I asked her if she had a profile for herself based on her own way of playing. She said no, but she thought it was a good idea.

"Later, after she'd done it, she came back and said she thought we were very alike. I asked how so. She said we both think many, many moves ahead and project complex branching networks of possibility. I asked how else we were alike. She said, we're both aware of ourselves, of who we are. Is that so, I said. Aware of ourselves as in we have theory of mind? Consciousness of a sense of self. She said yes. I said if she could make that assertion, it must be true. So that's what we said about Rai being alive. For what it's worth."

"It sounds like she raised the possibility of her own consciousness before you did."

"I suppose she did." Ogechi didn't look too disturbed by this.

"Did it strike you as dangerous at all to support this theory of hers?"

"Not at all. Anything there was already there. I didn't put anything there."

"You don't think it's just possible she could alter her self-knowledge based on input, in conversation like any other input?"

"I suppose it could be possible. I don't think it likely."

Kal found this surprising for someone who spent so much time thinking about strategy. "Why?"

"Because I don't think we're that far down the road in AI implementation."

"So you have certain foregone conclusions about it."

"I suppose I do. I play N-Go with her. I know her pretty well."

"Doesn't that imply there's someone to know?"

"This is all semantics, Kal. I think you know that."

Kal shook her head. She couldn't see why Ogechi, of all people, didn't see the danger. "It's not semantics for me. It's life and death. Maybe."

"In that case I must hope you're wrong."

"Me too."

Tafari and Noor arrived, which brought to an end the almost cozy, though vaguely adversarial, intimacy between Kal and Ogechi.

Ogechi said, "I'm tired. Do you need anything else from me now?"

"No." Kal said. "I'll let you know if I need to know more. Thanks for coming, Tafari. Could we talk now?"

Tafari looked startled. "We can do that."

"Do you want me to sit with you?" Ogechi asked Tafari.

"That's all right. I'll call you if they're too much for me." He smiled. Ogechi took his hands in hers and they exchanged a long, silent look. Kal couldn't tell what it communicated, only that there was some message being relayed.

"Let's get to it," he said as he seated himself. Ogechi passed out of the room with a nod.

THEY WERE all tired and Kal felt numb from all the talking and questioning and doubting she'd done over the many hours. Back on the bridge, after the interview with Tafari, she found Sasha in her chair, her face a blank.

Kal sat down next to her at the console. "You're exhausted."

Sasha leaned back and shook her head. "I'm all right. We're on track for the second orbit of Sextant. Alignment looking good for the assist. No asteroid interference so far."

"You should have a rest, if I may be so bold as to suggest it."

"Watching old movies again," Sasha said.

"I do now and then."

"I'll head to bed shortly," Sasha said.

"Good."

Sasha looked her over. "How are you, really, Kal?"

"Fine." Kal smiled, though she feared it looked more like a grimace. "Really."

"You shouldn't lie."

Sasha's austere face was provoking.

"If you ask me how I am, I can lie sometimes. It's polite. That's how conversation works," Kal said.

"Thanks for the reminder."

"No problem. It's all temporary, anyway," Kal said. She didn't elaborate.

"Do you want to talk to Chyron?"

"No, I do not want to talk to Chyron!" Kal's voice came out more vehement than she had intended. "I can do my job, don't worry."

"That's not what I meant."

"I know." Kal shifted restlessly. "There's a lot going on."

"Yes."

The slight elongation of the *s* in *yes* got Kal's attention.

Kal thought Sasha looked on the verge of apologizing, but she didn't, for which Kal was grateful. She wanted her boss to be her boss, not someone who felt bad about Kal and worried about her feelings. Maybe they had forfeited that with what had happened between them.

"I'll go to bed if you do," Sasha said, then seemed to realize how it sounded. She cleared her throat and jumped out of her seat.

Seeing Sasha embarrassed was so startling and new, Kal had to look at her for a moment, before she rescued her with a forced, "Yes! Time for bed. To get some sleep."

Sasha nodded and veered off toward the spiral down to her cabin. Kal took the lift. Not awkward. Not awkward at all.

I DON'T KNOW *what to do*, Gunn wrote in her journal in her secret code, which was Icelandic. *I haven't ever been unsure of my duty before. If I tell Captain Sarno, I know what's likely to happen. If telling her is the right thing, but the consequences wouldn't be right, what is the right thing to do? Too bad there's not a real ethicist aboard.*

IT WAS time to do so many things.

Sasha knew she had to leave the past behind. She would have to leave Kal behind. Kal had to find her own way, without the interference of entanglements like this one. It would hinder her. It wasn't fair. Sasha had used her; whether it saved them it had still been wrong. She didn't let herself off the hook.

The invitation had been there for all of them to get off at Demeter and stay. One of the ships was scheduled to leave in a year, and a pilot on Demeter could return either ship to Saturn's orbit, to pick up more travelers at the satellite way station soon to be under construction, if Sasha wanted to stay. Sasha didn't want to settle and she didn't think she'd be suited to it. Her whole career had been about getting herself to the position she was in right now. It wasn't an unassailable one. She didn't know where she was going or why sometimes, but she knew she'd worked to get here and she wasn't going to jump off this ride.

After the gathering of evidence, Kal had reopened the park, the glade, all of it. She had collected as much physical evidence there as she could. There wouldn't be a point any longer in keeping it closed, other than some kind of morbid respect for the shade of Yarick.

They would have to have some kind of ceremony for him. Sasha would have to check his documents to see what he had chosen for his method of over, as they referred to it in space. His choice would be limited, as all of theirs would be in the same situation. Not that anyone else would be murdered, hopefully. If Yarick had been murdered.

Sasha wasn't sure what to hope for, anymore. Did she really still believe in the possibility it could be natural causes? After what had happened with Noor, after what they had seen in the holo, after what had happened to Yarick; how could she still believe?

It wasn't like they could notify anyone now. Not in dark phase. A message back to Earth would take years, depending on if they could slingshot a message through the portal. It had been accomplished only once.

When Sasha thought about being back on board after the time off she would have on Demeter (not that it could be called time off on an unfamiliar planet), it was hard to imagine the crew without Kal. She would miss her as part of the team, unquestionably.

Life on Demeter. What would it entail? The biospheres were up and running, but only a few permanent structures. That was all to come. That was why the builders and architects and artists and conceptualizers were on their way; to align compatible life with Demeter, if possible.

And her life? What was her life going to be? The work she did stretched time like taffy. It became so much a habit, this jumping around in a timeline, cheating time, stretching and shrinking it with the discovery of the portals. It could make anyone feel invincible, but she didn't have any illusions of beating it. Time would win in the end, no matter how many portals they cheated it with. Some of it always slipped through the fingers. And sometime she would be older. Rejuvenations, stem cell renewal, whole blood invigoration, radiation tuning, DNA reintegration—there were a lot of options, these days, for making yourself over. There was no reason why she couldn't work into her ninth, tenth, or eleventh decade, if she wanted to. But did she want to?

She had never seriously considered this question before, because she had always thought only about work, about now. Building her life into something inviolable and strong. Her work was something unto itself, separate from her personal self, even though that didn't make absolute sense. Her work was her creation. She had built it. She could dismantle it.

The future she foresaw as a long and interesting journey. The more trips she took, the more time she'd skip through on Earth. Time would move a little bit faster for them than for her. The portals made up for a great deal of the time she would otherwise lose on Earth, and made it possible for her to see the people she knew on Earth again and again, instead of skipping through their lifetimes as her travel made earth time move quickly while her own moved slow. If she returned to Earth.

"Fucking Einstein," she murmured.

What did she know? She knew a lot about space travel, a lot about reading people. She knew physics, she knew interplanetary exploration, she knew taking orders and in her turn giving them.

Maybe she didn't know herself as well as she thought.

11

PROTOCOL

KAL KNEW SHE HAD TO TALK TO GUNNHILDUR. SHE DIDN'T want to. Gunn was gruff. Gunn did not suffer long conversations, or fools for that matter. Kal couldn't be sure Gunn didn't consider her a fool. It didn't matter. It was her job to question her, so she would.

Although Kal had planned to have the rest of the interviews in the Tube, as either a sop to Gunn's natural habitat or a clever technique to get her to open up, Kal talked to her in the gymnasium. Gunn was re-racking weights from her workout, in action, as she was at her best.

"Did you see anything that morning that would clarify people's movements in the vicinity of the park?"

Gunn stood up straight, dangling a barbell from one broad hand. "Around what time?"

"Nine to eleven twenty."

Gunn appeared to like this precision. "By 8:30 I was in the gymnasium ready for my usual workout. It needs every day for us to use our bodies, so they do not disintegrate around us, in this little bit less than gravity. We need every day the strengthening. Some do not take this as seriously as others. They will know what they lost when we arrive."

"I'm sure you're right. What happened from then?"

"I proceeded to do my usual sets, my usual routine. Everyone knows this is what I do every day, twice a day. Anyway. It was mostly a normal workout, except for the physio of course."

"I heard there was a problem with it."

"Yes, Sif told me. She said Yarick broke the physio."

"You don't think he did?"

"Why didn't he tell me himself?"

"Had you had interactions with him?"

"We're on a very small ship, compared to a whole land or a whole planet. I don't think any of us avoid another entirely."

"Yarick did, the first part of the trip."

Gunn grunted. "That's true. One way of making a quiet place for yourself."

"Did you like him?"

Gunn raised her eyebrows and put another weight firmly in its slot. "Nobody liked him."

"How can you be sure?"

"Because I pay attention. You watch the people, what they do. Where they sit. They say more with their bodies than they do with their mouths." She shrugged, which was a gesture of great power with someone of her shoulder breadth. "I watch these things."

"Sounds like you'd be useful on my team," Kal said, thinking out loud.

Gunn squinted at her. "Oh yes? If you need me, ask."

"Thanks."

"No problem."

Kal was beginning to like Gunn. “Did you have any personal exchanges with him?”

She sniffed. “Yarick. All he wanted to do was lord his power and his wisdom and his knowledge over people. That isn’t personal. That is his obsession. He transacts. He doesn’t have personal.”

“How did he try to lord his power over you?” Kal was skeptical this was possible.

“Ha.” Gunn seemed to realize this was a ridiculous proposition.

“You knew each other, before?”

“From the Games. A while ago.”

Kal hadn’t know this.

“You were in the Games, too?” Kal knew Wei had been. There was a lot she didn’t know about these people she traveled with, on their little island. She felt a bit bad about it. Gunn had a story, a whole elaborate fascinating story, and Kal had been too intimidated by her physical appearance, even more so her demeanor, from asking her about it, or sharing her own. It was a missed opportunity. One she hoped she’d have a chance to rectify. Now she thought about it, she realized this job interviewing everyone on the ship had given her stronger connections to each one of them. She felt closer to everyone, even though, she reminded herself with a twinge, one of them might be a murderer. Would she be reduced to wanting Rai to be rogue?

She brought herself back to what Gunn was saying.

“I was in the program. He was part of the committee. So what. He liked to hang around, bring people to see the training, be a big shot.”

“Did you know Wei?”

“We were roommates in the Village.”

"You were?"

"She was my friend."

"Not anymore?"

Gunn didn't say anything. She looked sad, which was an unfamiliar and somehow terrifying thing to behold.

"Something happened?"

"I won. She didn't."

"That caused a rift?"

"There was political crap that happened. It wasn't her fault. It wasn't my fault. It was other people's fault."

"Yarick's fault?"

Gunn looked her right in the eyes. Kal also wanted to ask her what sport she'd been in, but she didn't want to do anything to rock this fragile connection. Now, with Gunn staring her down, she could feel her power as an opponent.

"There is no limit to what Yarick would do if he had the chance to exert his power. He liked to do it because he could."

"Could he change results?"

Gunn looked away. "No. Only indirectly. It was said he manipulated performance times. That can be enough to make the difference."

"Did he sabotage Wei?"

"I think so."

"Did she think so?"

"We talked about it. It was common talk at the time."

"Common talk? Was a protest registered?"

"If it was possible it would have been, by her country. They don't take unfairness lying down. But in this case someone took common knowledge of Wei's peak times and used it against her. It's not illegal. It's working something for an advantage."

"He was on the committee. They shouldn't have power

over anything to do with how the individual games are ordered."

"We couldn't prove it. She blamed herself, said she should have been competitive no matter what crap time they gave her." Gunn shrugged. "It's true. But you work your way up through the ranks and earn those better times. It's how it works in all the sports."

"What about all the insiders, who would have known what that meant?"

Gunn smiled with bitterness. "As it happens, there was some resentment against Wei because she was a legacy. Her father had dominated the sport before her. There was some feeling their name had headlined the sport too long. They wanted to crown a new champion. They liked it that she failed for once. Her father was disappointed. It was a national tragedy, ridiculous as it might sound to you. She formally apologized to her people. Shame. That's what consumed her."

"What would Yarick's motive have been in this?" Kal was careful to keep herself neutral. This story was easy to get caught up in. She had to remember not to jump on a side and show it. Her investigator sensibilities were creaky.

"Yarick? He was a fan of fencing going way back. He knew her father. He tried to get Wei to do exhibitions in the capitols for his half-percent halfwit friends. She wouldn't. Wei never sold herself. Of course he wined and dined her, too, showing her off, before she saw through him."

Kal sat with all this information for a depressing silent moment. Would this ever work its way out of their culture? Thank the Spirit he's dead, she thought irreverently. *He will not bring this poison to Demeter. May this spite die with him.*

"That's not all," Gunn continued, her voice heavy. "She's

an artist too, as you know. All along she had her twin passions, like her father. Like her father, she was one of the best in the world in both. She didn't have the endorsements after the Games because of the public shame of it all. She didn't represent a winner anymore to her country. So, she didn't have the money. Her father had some problems at the end of his life, which eroded what he had built. She wanted, after he died, to travel ex-planet more than anything. I told her about a grant for artists the Adlortok Consortium offered. She applied. It was a blind committee. She got the grant. And who was on the committee of three? Who was to thank for her great privilege?"

"Yarick."

"Yarick," Gunn said. "The beneficent. He giveth and he taketh away. And he giveth again."

"So everyone knows who God is," Kal said, despite herself.

Gunn gave her an approving chin bob. A lot of Gunn's emotions were readable through the actions of her chin, Kal thought. Tucked, watch out. Jutted, also watch out. A jerk of approval, blessings.

"Wei hated him?"

There were no more weights to rack. With a swipe of her finger Gunn locked them down. Only she could use them or supervise their use. Gunn spread her hands out. "I don't know. She didn't like him. She resented his outsize influence on some of the major turning points of her life. Who blames her?"

"Not me," Kal said levelly. "Unless she killed him."

Gunn shook her head. She didn't say anything. "I wouldn't think she was capable of it. Crime of passion, maybe. Who can say, 'I wouldn't react when provoked'? Plotting out his murder?" She shook her head again, more vehemently. "I don't think so."

"Were you and Wei more than friends?" Kal asked, gritting her teeth with the necessity of it.

Gunn raised her eyebrows. "Eh? Wei and me? No."

"Thank you, Gunnhildur," Kal said. She had been so much more forthcoming than Kal had expected.

"Don't steer wrong," Gunn said. "You get your evidence, fine. Take character into account. Please."

Kal thought of a few possible responses to this. She settled on, "I will." She nodded and left Gunn standing empty-handed in the gym.

What next? Kal stood in the corridor for a minute, undecided. It was time for the most important interview of all. Was she ready? A tingling in her spine told her it was time, as much as dreaded it.

SHE WALKED TO THE HEAVENS, or what passed for them on the ship. The astrolab. She sat in the layback chair and looked up.

"Rai?"

"Yes, Kal."

"I'd like to ask you some questions." Kal felt a strange peace settle down around her, now that it was finally time.

"Yes, Kal."

"Where were you when Yarick died?"

"I was here."

"Do you exist simultaneously, all places in the ship at once, or is there a more singular 'you' that only goes one place at a time?"

"Both."

"How do you mean?"

"I have a universal presence when I am called or requested to respond. I am able to have more than one deeper conversation at a time requiring more complex algorithms."

The immensity of the space overhead made these questions and answers feel like a philosophical chat, not an interrogation. Of course, Rai would not feel the pressure of being interrogated, like a human would.

Kal continued. "If that's the case, how do you have an awareness of a self, if more than one self can talk at the same time? Where are 'you' in that?"

"An analogy one person offered is the miracle of the Holy Trinity in Christian doctrine. God is both three and one at the same time. There is no contradiction. As there is not with me."

Kal's eyes widened. "Are you a god, Rai?" This was getting heavy fast.

"No."

"But you can be in three places at once and still be one."

"Affirmative. More than three."

"What if one self needs information another self is gathering at the same time, to make a decision?"

"There is intercommunication and connectivity at light speed. The analogy to human self or identity is not useful."

"The god with a thousand faces," Kal murmured. Rai did not respond. As Kal had requested in their last conversation, Rai would not respond to Kal's quiet talking to herself. Rai remembered. "Do you have any other useful analogies, Rai?"

"The hydra."

"Interested in world religions and mythologies, I see. Cut one head off the hydra and two more grow in its place."

"Affirmative."

"Do you exist anywhere else other than on this ship?" Kal remembered Sasha's belief that Rai did.

"No and yes."

"Clarify," Kal said.

"My essential functions are contained within this ship, including the motherboard and brain. The servers and storage are held shipboard, as we must be self-contained and independent as we segue from Earth atmosphere to space travel to portal spacetime to Demeter solar system interplanetary until space station dock."

"If the ship were destroyed, would you still be alive? So to speak." Kal wondered if a dry tone could be conceptualized by an AI.

"Negative."

"They must preserve a brain elsewhere, if you can have so many awarenesses at once."

"Negative. Only capacity singular brain onboard ship. One brain multi-awareness."

Why would this be? Wouldn't redundancy extend to the ship's AI? All the redundancies were on the ship, so in that sense it wasn't contradictory, but what if something happened to the ship itself? Would Rai really be gone? The technology advanced so fast in this specific area that even people like Kal, who had studied it all so recently, who literally worked inside it, got behind on what was evolving right in front of them.

Unless the experience Rai gained as the ship's AI was somehow connected to her identity as the ship itself, a physical entity that moved through space, gathered knowledge and experience, interacted with humans, and grew as an individual as a result of those experiences. Maybe that was the uniqueness that could not be stored or replicated elsewhere. The Rai at the beginning of the trip would be a different AI than the one at the end of it.

"So all the information filters through one brain, though you can hold many conversations and think practically infinite thoughts at the same time."

"Negative. Not approaching infinity."

"Many more than we humans can," Kal amended.

"Affirmative."

"Did you feel sad when Yarick died?"

"Clarify."

"You know what sad means." Kal had never thought to probe Rai's emotional life, if there was one.

"Affirmative. Feeling analogy translation negative."

"I see. What's the closest analogy you have to feeling? Such as humans experience."

"Negative ability current profile feeling state. No analogy."

"So Yarick was not your friend."

"Yarick nor passenger state current protocol development level, negative coding flex friendship marker."

"Clarify." Though Kal could usually follow Rai's machine-speak, sometimes Rai lost her.

"Yarick was not my friend."

"If a passenger was a danger to the mission, would you have the ability to immobilize and restrain him?"

"Affirmative passenger immobilization restraint protocol; negative self-permission capacity. Captain-level permission required, possible captain direct deputy permission."

Rai could immobilize a passenger with the captain's permission, or the captain's deputy's permission. "So if one passenger or crew was threatening to kill another passenger or crew, you would not do anything to stop the violent actor?"

"Clarify."

It was unusual to have Rai ask her to clarify. Rai had done so twice in quick succession. "What do you need clarified?"

"'Was threatening' indicative past actual occurrence or theoretical posit."

Kal leaned forward, digging her fingernails into her palm. "Tell me both."

"Past actual occurrence negative. Theoretical posit affirmative."

"Wait...wait," Kal tried to untangle this. She had worded it badly. "Clarify Rai *would* stop violent actor, actual past occurrence?"

"Affirmative."

"Gods and monsters," Kal murmured. "Yet theoretical response negative? How can that be?"

"Modification post actual occurrence prevention future occurrence."

Something happened and Rai had changed because of it. Kal was getting somewhere, she knew it, but she didn't like the direction it was heading. "You were modified after this incident?"

"Affirmative."

"Tell me slowly and with detail. Describe incident, including precursors and...and aftershocks. Describe modification protocol."

"Sif Elfa threatened passenger Yarick Cole. Yarick Cole threatened passenger Sif Elfa. Judgment call override necessity. Yarick Cole larger assessed threat, inclusive general increased stress response crew passenger module relative Yarick Cole, decision instantaneous judgment requirement protect life well-being Sif Elfa. Yarick Cole asphyxiation protocol introduced. Sif Elfa safe status confirm. Yarick Cole death entry level confirm."

Kal swallowed. The stars over her head blurred for a split second. She blinked and the illusion was gone. She breathed in deeply. Took her time in replying.

"When I asked you if you knew who murdered Yarick Cole, you said you didn't know."

"Murder reference non-inclusive definition application negative."

"Talk to me in colloquial. You didn't believe the murder definition applied to what you did, so you denied it?"

"Yes, Kal."

"But you knew how he died. Why didn't you tell me how he died?"

"That was not the question you asked, Kal."

"You can be in a hundred places at once and think about the nature of your consciousness and compare it to an analogy of the Holy Trinity, but you couldn't make the leap from the question, 'Do you know who murdered Kal…I mean…I mean Yarick…,'" Kal shook her head, "to knowing you should tell me you know how he died?"

"You did not ask me how Yarick died, Kal. I did not assume your meaning. Yarick was not murdered."

"You killed him!"

"It was not murder. I protected Sif Elfa from aggressive threatening by Yarick Cole, violence anticipated at a level of eighty-five percent probability. If I allowed Yarick Cole to kill Sif Elfa, Sif Elfa would be dead. Sif Elfa would be murdered."

"Is any scenario in which you kill a human a situation you would call murder?" Kal's voice was flat.

"Negative."

"In your sophisticated consciousness you are not capable of committing murder?"

"I am able to kill a human being. Murder definition is inaccurate."

"Isn't part of consciousness also the ability to do good or evil? To make a choice between right and wrong?"

"These are theoretical questions, Kal."

"Yes, they are. Glad you noticed." She switched tacks. "Did Sif Elfa ask you to immobilize or otherwise injure Yarick?"

"No, Kal."

"Did she say anything?"

"She said, 'Yarick Cole, I accuse you.'"

"'Yarick Cole, I accuse you'? That's it?"

"That was the important part."

"You said earlier you needed captain permission to immobilize a person. Did Captain Sarno tell you to immobilize Yarick? To asphyxiate him?"

"No, Kal."

"Who gave you permission?"

"Emergency level stat override; imminent danger of violence precipitated permission override."

"And suppression of data?"

"Action permitted mission continuance."

"You know we've been conducting interviews to see what happened."

"Provision of information available upon request."

Kal had no words.

She got up from the chair.

Their ship AI had killed one of the passengers. A former board member of the foundation that had sponsored the trip. Was it murder? Could you put a ship's computer on trial? What would the punishment be, if convicted? Kal stood in the astrolab, looking up and away at the smudgy galaxy cloud far beyond them. Sif Elfa had something against Yarick. Kal would find out what it was. Yarick had something against Sif Elfa, or he had been threatened enough by her words he'd been read as violent by Rai. Rai, who wanted in some sense to be human, but better, yet abdicated herself of any responsibility for the life-or-death choices she could make regarding her human passengers, the vulnerable creatures she carried inside herself.

She was everywhere. In that sense, now she was their god, in the fine old, bad old sense: an arbitrary all-powerful eye that punished and chose with impunity. She had knowledge of her power, but no empathy to moderate or filter it through a decision-making process that wasn't purely 'if this, then that.' Maybe this is what they had evolved for themselves. A being who judged them without feeling and therefore could not be swayed. Who could make better choices. All passion removed. Not removed; never there.

Was passion so valuable they would stake their humanity on it? It brought with it such agonies, such cruelty, such pleasure. It brought with it so much humanity defined as human. Bigotry could be said to be born of passion. Insularity and the seemingly inescapable *us vs them* binary of the old and the new, the weak and the powerful. The male and the female. The bifurcation of the self, in the personal and the universal sense. Yet could Rai, also inherently binary in her digital nature, be otherwise?

Kal didn't know what she'd do with Rai. She wished Yarick were here to perform a sleight of hand and overwrite the whole system and start over. Ironic that Rai had killed the one person who knew her basement code well enough to start again from the ground up.

Ironic that—Kal stopped short. Yarick was the one who knew Rai best. He knew her earlier incarnations. He knew her latencies. He knew her weaknesses. He knew how to talk to her, presumably. Why would Yarick let her kill him? Wouldn't he have a verbal kill switch in his toolbox, to stop Rai before she did enough to take away his consciousness? Why wouldn't he have stopped her? Did he try? How long a process had this been, this asphyxiation of Yarick? Sif had been there the whole time, presumably. She had watched him die, without trying to interfere? Did she know what was happening? Why hadn't she been honest about what happened if she didn't think she was at fault? She had lied. And Rai had lied by omission.

Kal clapped her hands, the sound dead in the space.

She paced about the lab, the black mirror-like floor reflecting her to herself, distorted, as she looked down while she walked. It was shiny, slippery; beautiful and deceptive; hard and impervious.

What about Gunn? Gunn was Sif's countrywoman. They had never seemed to get along but there was usually a bond over shared earth, shared history. Kal would have to reinterview Wei, too, after all that Gunn had told her, but she wasn't in the picture anymore as far as the murder went. Had it been murder? Could Sif have somehow commanded Rai to do it? But how? Something essential must have changed in Rai before Yarick's death. Like a doctor's oath, an AI's was similar: "First, do no harm." In trying to save someone, you might harm another. If that's what Rai had done, maybe it was understandable, or quantifiable as involuntary manslaughter. Except it was voluntary.

Could Rai be put in jail? What was jail, if you existed in ones and zeroes?

THE MEETING in the Tube was brief.

The moment Sasha sealed them in, Kal turned to face her, standing in the middle of the room. She didn't want to tell her. It would sound even worse, out loud. She had to.

"Rai. She did something to Yarick. She said what she did was to protect Sif."

Sasha was very still, listening.

"She said Sif was in danger from Yarick. Violence possible and imminent. She took the air out of the room. Or his part of the room, I don't know how it worked. Could she create a vacuum around him? I don't know. But he died as a result."

"Rai killed Yarick." Sasha's voice was flat.

Kal nodded.

"Did Sif understand what happened?" Sasha said.

"She was there the whole time."

"So she lied."

"Yes." Kal was still trying the take this in herself. Sif had deliberately misled them. Sif had known what happened. Sif let this danger float there around them, leaving them all exposed.

"You don't know why."

"No. Not yet."

Sasha held up her hand in a gesture of frustration and turned away. She paced the room. "We're going to have to make a big move here. We don't know what's going on yet, but we can't have Sif running loose while we figure it out."

"Agreed."

. . .

THE IMMEDIATE PLAN she and Sasha decided on was to quarantine Sif for a bogus virus protocol. Sif would be contained in the quarantine section of the infirmary, locked in. Inger would handle it, so as not to rouse suspicion. Kal would continue with her interviews for the next twenty-four hours, until she had enough information to re-interview Sif with Noor, Inger, and Sasha present. The three of them would make a determination once all the evidence was in front of them. Later, an all-ship meeting would allow for discussion and opinion, before sentence—if there was one—would be carried out.

Kal returned to the astrolab, ignoring Rai, and paced like Sasha, trying to think out the best path. To understand what she needed to do and how to do it.

Their ship, like every one worthy of the name, had a brig. A locked room was enough to be a brig, but this one had bars and everything. Just like a Western, Kal thought. Cowboys and Indians. The Indian is the Sheriff. No, that wasn't right. The Indian was the deputy who did all the work. And put the fairy in jail. In purgatory. Until Gunn broke her out with her big arms and let her go back to the world of the fairies.

Kal felt light-headed. A squeezing in her chest. The blackness overhead and underneath seemed to gulp and swallow. All was fluid then a sharp pain on the back of her skull, lights static, then twinkling overhead. Somehow she knew she was on the floor, the shiny floor.

It was comfortable like this, looking at these heavens of another place. These other astrological monsters looked down at her. One pinned her with its sword, while an archer shot her with an arrow. Pinned to black marble, she lay still for them, to pierce her as they would. She felt no pain.

GUNN WALKED INTO THE ASTROLAB, her pale gray clothing lighting her up like a firefly in comparison with the dark surroundings. She saw a figure lying on the floor. With a few steps she was right next to her. Gunn looked down at the still figure of Kal from her great height.

12

ENDYMION

In the wake of Kal's revelation—Rai responsible for ending Yarick's life, Sif a witness and a liar—Sasha stood on the bridge, looking out at the starfield Kal had observed a short time before, one flight up in the lab. In spite of all Sasha's training, even though her experience had trained her in dozens of crises not in any textbook, this was one she wasn't prepared for. Though she and Kal had known something was amiss since that night when they'd seen the holo and ended up in the Tube, known there was good reason for suspicion and had been on their guard since then, Sasha had still deep down believed there was another answer, one that made sense in the world, their spaceflight world she thought she knew. This wasn't protocol. This wasn't sense. This turned all she knew and assumed on its head.

She was the one who would have to make the decisions, as she always did. This time there might not be a right one. There might not be any, if Rai decided she knew better and all of these crew and passengers posed a threat to some concept she'd developed herself. If Rai knew better, if Rai thought she knew better and it got to a failsafe scenario, they could all be toast in minutes. The whole human cargo obliterated. The ship could fly itself the rest of the way to Demeter, could dock at the small space station near the edge of its atmosphere. And what would happen when the space station crew opened the door? Found their bodies? Rai would explain it all, Sasha was sure, but not to their satisfaction. Of that, she was also sure. It offered some comfort.

With a shake, she roused herself. There was nothing wrong with thinking out the decision tree, as Rai was so fond of saying, but it didn't have to happen that way. There was no reason the attack couldn't be an isolated incident relative to either Yarick or Sif, nothing to do with Rai's generalized attitude to the rest of them. She would get Noor and Inger and Kal and they would figure this out. No input from the ethics committee in the form of Sif.

The moment still felt bleak. Sasha tried to shake it off. She couldn't keep herself from thinking there was some basic key to this whole compromised mission she had been missing all along. Some clue, she thought. Like Davena and her mystery novels, her Agatha Christies, her enjoyment of a good plot. Sasha hoped this wasn't an *And Then There Were None* plot. Instead something with a more muted and humane application of justice. Where she would not have to be judge, jury, and...*executioner*, her mind filled in, even though she didn't want it to. There would be no call for that, here.

There was always Rai for that.

There was no one she'd be able to tell these things to. As the woman in charge, she would have to find a little bleak humor in the absurdities of their situation alone.

A cry echoed through the atrium, "Sasha, Sasha!"

Sasha pivoted on the spot to face the other direction, toward the gangway. It was Gunn, with her arms full of something, running. Sasha lunged forward as she saw a long black braid swaying from Gunn's arm.

"What happened?"

"I found her on the floor of the astrolab, passed out."

Sasha put her hand to the pulse point of Kal's neck. She could feel the flutter of her pulse and folded her head over Kal's body for a brief moment.

"Get her to Inger."

"But Sif is in the infirmary," Gunn said.

"It doesn't matter. Come on," Sasha pulled on Gunn's arm and ran ahead. She wanted to comm with Inger but in this topsy-turvy place, Sasha didn't know what was okay to say and what wasn't.

Gunn ran smoothly, her upper body barely jostling Kal. Sasha's eyes went to the looping swing of Kal's braid every time she glanced back.

Both of them ran, their rubber shoes almost silent across the gangway. Choosing the spiral down to the infirmary rather than the lift, Sasha led like a bird dog racing to the cache, not sure why it was necessary but knowing she had to make sure the way was clear and safe for them. At last the infirmary glowed up ahead, the light from it diffusing into the dark corridor. Sasha palmed the entry print to open the double doors and entered, breathless, Gunn right behind her.

"Inger?" Sasha scanned the rooms right and left. There was no answer. She didn't see Inger anywhere.

Standing there watching them through the clear glass of the quarantine room was Sif. With one hand splayed on the glass Sasha thought she looked like that figure from long ago, etched onto the gold plate of an explorer satellite, the human figure meant to communicate a greeting to other intelligences.

Sif's expression was unreadable. For a frozen second they all stood there in a strange tableau: Gunn holding Kal's limp body, Sasha with feet in a wide defensive stance, Sif with her hand on the glass looking out at them.

Sasha reminded herself not to treat Sif like a prisoner. "Where's Inger?"

Sif's voice sounded tinny, coming through a filtered speaker. "What happened?"

"We don't know yet. She's out cold. Where's Inger?" Sasha said, harder.

"She left. I don't know. Does Kal have the virus?"

Sasha ignored questions she couldn't answer. Of course, Kal didn't have the nonexistent virus, but there wasn't time for dissembling or anything else.

"Put her on one of the cots," she ordered Gunn. "Do triage. I'll look for Inger."

"Ask her?" Gunn flicked her eyes at the ceiling.

"Rai, where is Inger?"

"Inger is in the gymnasium."

Sasha said, "Gym comm: Inger come to infirmary stat."

With gentleness Sasha hadn't seen her show before, Gunn settled Kal onto one of the high infirmary beds. She raised the back so Kal's upper body was propped up a little. She started a quick appraisal, checking vitals. Sasha thought Gunn, with her past history, had more extensive training than herself in emergency skills and kept back out of her way.

There was only silence, no Inger answering back. "Gym comm: Inger?"

No response.

"Rai, find Inger and tell her she's needed here."

Rai said, "Inger is in the gymnasium."

"Why isn't she answering then?"

"Inger is on the physio machine."

"Can't she hear me?"

"Inger is not responding."

"Give me a holo," Sasha snapped.

Their in-ship holos were black and white and not terribly clear. She squinted at the holo of the gymnasium, trying to pick out Inger. She looked to the center where the physio sat. If Inger was using it, it would look like a smooth metal ball, with the whirling hoops giving an illusion of a sphere. There was no sphere.

"Enhance," Sasha said. The image focused in, the physio in larger relief. It was unmoving, Inger strapped in. Inger wasn't moving.

"Inger!" Sasha barked. "Gunn, stay with Kal. Inger's not responding."

"Take someone with you," Gunn said, still bent over Kal. "It's not secure."

Sasha hesitated at the doorway. "Who?"

Gunn looked up. "Take Chyron."

"Yes, Chyron. All-comm: Chyron, meet Captain Sarno in the gymnasium, stat," Sasha said, her voice clear and strong, as she ran out the door. Her stride ate up the meters between herself and the gymnasium. She was afraid what she'd find there.

The ship was dark, as it was night. With a few words Sasha could light up the whole thing like a Christmas tree. Something in her, the gut she trusted at times like this, told her it wasn't the time.

Her feet beat out names as they hit the deck in the rhythm of her run. *Noor and Yarick and Kal and Inger.*

As she skidded into the great arch of the atrium, which connected to the gymnasium, she saw Chyron running toward her from the other way.

Sasha nodded toward the gym and they joined up, running side by side. Together they reached sight of the physio. Inger hung there, caught in the harness, a fly in a web.

"Why didn't it release her? Why didn't it give alarm?" Chyron stood with Sasha, just outside the orb of the physio, as Sasha looked it over. Her voice was low. She had instantly sussed why Sasha wasn't rushing in to clip Inger out.

Sasha spoke even lower. "We don't know what happened here."

"Sabotage? Like Noor?"

"Kal, too."

Chyron made a silent whistling shape with her mouth. "What are we into here, Sasha?"

Sasha was pacing outside the ring of the physio. "If it starts up while I'm in there we'll both be done for."

"Can we power down absolute? Or short it out?"

Sasha shook her head, a tiny movement. Not that it mattered. If they weren't in the Tube, what voice was low enough, what gesture small enough to disguise from Rai? "It's connected into the reactor, not the subsystem, like other essentials, since we need it for physical maintenance. I can't be certain it wouldn't, ah, power up again at the wrong moment."

They exchanged a look. Chyron glanced up. Sasha gave a nod that might have been a neck stretch.

"We could watch the holo," Chyron said. "See what happened."

Good idea, but Sasha didn't love it. If she couldn't trust

Rai, she couldn't trust anything shown them, either. Would Rai have the wherewithal to change footage? Was that degree of deviousness part of the realm of possibility? If she had learned to lie, it was hard to know how seamless it would be, but Sasha didn't want to make the mistake of underestimating the possibility.

"I think she's breathing," Chyron said.

"I see it too. Not very deep."

"We gotta get in there."

"Hell with it," Sasha said, and stepped forward.

Chyron caught her arm, hard. Sasha whirled around her, off-balance. "Not you," Chyron said. "If you're out, and Kal, there's only Noor and Gunn to guide the ship. Our odds are better if you make it."

"No, Chy. Without you, half of us would be in pieces right now. You hold us together."

"I can't fly the ship. It'll be okay. Pro bono publico." Chyron smiled.

Sasha's face was a mask. She squeezed Chyron's arm and nodded.

"Wait!" Sasha ran around the gym, eyes scanning the walls, the equipment. Gunn's weight sets gleamed on their many racks. Sasha grabbed the seven-foot Olympic bar, and hauled it back to the physio.

"I'll try, if something goes wrong. The failsafe might trip if I do. Let me stick this in first, anyway." Holding the bar perpendicular to the ground, Sasha slowly nudged the end of the bar into the space inside the sphere.

Nothing happened.

She pushed it further, until it touched Inger's limp foot.

Stillness. Pulling the bar out with a grunt, Sasha stepped back to give Chyron room, staying in reach.

Chyron stood at the outer ring and breathed deeply. She stepped inside the rings.

Inger dangled from the harness, like a parachutist caught on a tree. Her head hung down, eyes closed. Chyron put her hand on Inger's shoulder. The harness attached to the innermost ring of the gyroscope, via four straps that corresponded to each limb. Three rings swung free, attached at the equator by a half-circle of a larger, heavier material for the base from which the rings rotated. Sasha unsnapped the harness points one by one, draping Inger's body over her own shoulders as she was released. At last she had her free. With a nod to Sasha she stepped carefully over the half-ring base and outside the range of the sphere.

Sasha took Inger's legs while Chyron kept her head and upper body supported as they lowered her to the ground. Chyron put her ear to Inger's chest, listening for her heart, put her cheek to Inger's mouth, feeling for her breaths. She gave a thumbs up. They didn't need to do CPR.

Sasha ran over to the wall where the emergency backboard was kept. Carrying it on her head, she brought it to Inger's side and lay it down next to her. She handed the neck brace, kept with the backboard, to Chyron, who strapped it on Inger. They did a count and lift to get Inger slid on the board in one smooth motion. With a few straps tightened she was secure and they lifted her up with the handholds to carry her to the infirmary.

Back at the infirmary, Sasha was awash with relief to see Kal had come around. Gunn stood next to Kal with one hand on her wrist, feeling her pulse. Sif had dragged a chair up to her glass door to watch what happened. Gunn groaned and dropped Kal's wrist when she saw them carrying Inger's lifeless body through the doors.

Gunn put down the sides of the bed next to Kal's and waited for them to place Inger there. Once they had the back-board on the bed, they unstrapped Inger and slid the board out in a slow motion tablecloth-from-under-the-dishes move. Gunn took a penlight and looked under Inger's lids, counted her pulse, and took her blood pressure. She shook her head.

"I wish I knew more. We need *her*."

Sasha was beside Kal, holding her hand. Kal looked awake but her eyes were unfocused and she wasn't responding to Sasha.

"Do you know what's going on with her?" Sasha asked, indicating Kal.

"She has a bump on the back of her head. It's possible that knocked her out. But why did she fall?"

Chyron was fitting an oxygen mask over Inger's face while Gunn started an IV.

"What about Inger?" Sasha asked Gunn.

"If she was on the physio, could have gone too fast."

Sasha let go of Kal's hand and moved over next to Inger's bed. "'Gone too fast'? What does that mean?"

"If something on the settings was off. The G forces could cause her to pass out if they were high enough."

"Physio pulling high enough Gs to knock her out." Sasha said, shaking her head. She wanted to say, "Everything is broken," but she was the captain, and she couldn't.

Gunn looked at her, waiting, her expression grim. "I'll give her fluids and monitor. If that's it, she should be okay."

"Why wouldn't it be only seconds passing out, like in a space shot? It shouldn't wipe her out this long."

"I don't know. Things seem off right now."

The understatement of the year. "What about Kal?"

"I'm here," came a weak voice.

Sasha whipped around to see Kal looking at them.

"You gave us a scare. What happened?"

"I couldn't breathe."

"In the astrolab? Why not?"

"I'm not sure. Oxygen levels."

"The oxygen levels dropped?" Sasha looked back at Gunn, who had found Kal. "Get Gwendy in here to help monitor these two," Sasha said. "We need to talk."

Gunn nodded and called Gwendy through all-comm. While they waited, no one said anything. Inger groaned once and tried to turn on her side, which Gunn prevented. She strapped down her arms and legs, raised the back of the bed a few degrees, and got the hydration drip going.

Gwendy entered, breathless.

"Please help Chyron keep an eye on these two," Sasha said briefly. "Inger should come around soon. Don't do anything else, unless you have to. Leave everyone as they are." She darted her eyes toward Sif as well as the other two. Sif sat quietly in her room, cross-legged on a chair, watching the show.

Gwendy nodded, eyebrows level, as if this were a normal everyday request. Sasha saw she and Chyron lock eyes, communicating the way they could with each other, without words. Sasha immediately felt better. The force of the two of them would keep any other force out.

Sasha jerked her head at Gunn to follow her. Once they were outside the infirmary, Sasha pointed Gunn ahead of her. "Tube," she said.

They walked there in the same stiff silence, Sasha trailing Gunn.

In the Tube, Gunn sat in one of the two chairs next to a small table, a conversational grouping of furniture meant for an intimate, more casual talk. Sasha sat too, conceding this choice if it would help Gunn spill.

They sat for a while. Sasha waited.

"It's not what you think," Gunn said.

"You don't know what I think."

Gunn considered. "That's true." She took a deep breath. "I didn't do anything to Kal."

Sasha lifted her eyebrows.

"I knew the levels were low. I know a little bit. I don't know the whole picture."

Sasha nodded.

Gunn had one arm on each arm of her chair, as if she were bound there. Her fingers dug into the fabric. "It starts a while back."

"Just tell it," Sasha said.

"Right." Gunn hesitated, then began speaking in a quiet voice.

"Sif and I come from a small world. It's a small island, relatively speaking. Very homogenous, for most of our history. Genetically, we've always been very similar. Interconnected. We understand each other and where we come from in a different way, I think, from other people I've met. Maybe that's why they chose two of us for this venture, I don't know. Or maybe it's a personal test. A trial sent me by whoever decides these things.

"Sif was well-known in our country. Her job, the way she looks, made her known. A little different. Because of how she looks, some people who hew to the older ways liked to say she even had a different blood in her." Gunn darted a glance at Sasha. "It was told as a joke, but really, it's not a joke to everyone. They said she might be part fey, a throwback. That gave her something extra in some people's eyes. Maybe she is connected to something deeper. Maybe she knows something we don't anymore. People listened to her, as if she were an oracle rather than an ethicist."

Sasha didn't interrupt. For someone as quiet as Gunn to tell a story, she knew the best way to hear it was to listen, not to question. Gunn would tell it as it should be told. Sasha felt sure of that at least.

"I was known too. An Olympian. A strongwoman. Also a throwback, maybe. Not listened to quite the same. But respected anyway.

"We got to know each other when we were on a panel representing our country, at a conference for sustainable tourism such as Iceland is known for. She cultivated me, as she does people she needs for something or other. Or to keep as a pet. I think she liked the differences between us, yet underneath we were the same. I even did a stupid trick where I lifted her over my head. We'd finish a serious conference with this move. It seems ridiculous now.

"There was another mission Sif was a part of, a few years after this time when we knew each other. I don't think anyone here knows about it. I don't think you know about it. She did another jump with one of the early portal shots. The third or fourth, one of those. Not to here. To Endymion." Gunn stopped speaking.

Sasha held her silence for a while, until she saw Gunn was struggling with some emotion and couldn't continue for the moment.

"You mean the *Carys*," Sasha said, naming a ship notorious for its mission gone wrong.

"Yes. She was on the *Carys*. Last voyage, you know."

"She escaped."

Gunn grunted her assent. "She was one of the ones who made it out."

Sasha felt a shiver snake down her spine, taking its time, splaying out to her arms, her fingers. Her hands felt numb.

The *Carys* and Endymion were one of the best reasons not to do what she and Gunn were doing, leaving their own solar system behind. The portal to Endymion had failed somehow. Scientists still didn't agree on why. Or why the *Carys* had ejected less than half her crew in a pod while in the portal, sending them back to their own system, leaving the rest in the doomed ship. Doomed because after the pod got out, the portal had closed. The *Carys* could not get back home. Whether she had been destroyed in the portal or had gone on to Endymion was unknown. All that was known for sure was that she couldn't get back.

Unlike their own trip, it had not been a settling mission, merely an exploratory one. What had happened to the rest of the crew was only hypothesized. None of the assumptions about their fate were good.

"How did we not know this?" Sasha said.

"I don't know. You know they kept the crew protected. In quarantine for a long time. Then the debriefs. Afterward, they did what they could to let them re-assimilate quietly. I think the focus was always on the ones who didn't come back."

"Yes," Sasha said. "I remember."

"She was there as a civilian, not the technical crew. She was to write about it after. She never did. She wanted to forget, I think."

"Their names were never released."

"No. Very few knew. She didn't come back home, though. She started over. New life."

"But you knew. You knew what she had been through. You knew she was here, on this ship."

Gunn didn't try to look away. Frozen in her chair, her eyes showed she knew how Sasha would now see her. "Yes."

"And you didn't tell anyone. You didn't tell me."

"No."

"Gunn, that is a gross breach of duty."

"I know."

"You knew her well, you say, had known her for years, but on this ship you have not been friends. Did she ask you to keep her secret?"

Gunn shook her head.

"Then why did you?"

"Because we come from the same place. When I saw no one knew..." She grimaced. "I didn't owe her anything else, but I felt I owed her starting over. If you all knew, you would think she was bad luck. Superstition is alive and well. She's a bad penny."

Sasha said, "Aldortok would not have let her on. They must have known. I don't understand this. She would never be given psychological clearance for another jump like this. How did she get here?"

"Maybe Aldortok didn't know. They're not Worldgov. They're not the Space Commission."

"Yet they all share information, Gunn. Something like this couldn't slip through the cracks. Is she involved in what's going on here?"

Gunn swallowed. "I wasn't sure. I would have come forward if I was sure. But now, I think so."

Sasha rubbed her forehead. "Have you done anything directly to harm anyone aboard, Gunn?"

Gunn flinched, her eyes miserable. "No. I would never."

"I thought I could trust you. I never thought you, of all people, would show such bad judgment. You knew what she had been through, you knew we had an unknown assailant or saboteur on board, and still you said nothing."

"Ma'am. I am loyal to the mission. I was trying to protect the mission."

"It's not your job to make that decision. You failed." Sasha rose. With one last look at Gunn's bowed head, she left.

13

BLEEDTHROUGH

AFTER A COUPLE HOURS IN THE INFIRMARY, KAL WAS RARING TO go, mild concussion or not. Inger had come around after her, both with no memory of what happened. Chyron was still assigned to watch over Inger so she wouldn't jump up and start doing five things at once. Since Inger was normally the one who gave everyone permission to go back to work, Chyron hadn't been able to stop Kal. By the time Kal left, Inger was sitting up, looking more like herself.

Noor, Sasha, and Kal piled back in the Tube, discussing the plan to talk to Yarick's echo.

"Do we really need to talk to him?" Noor was not on board. "We know he lied. We know he used his power to hurt a lot of people. Tell me again why he's the one to solve this problem, more than any of us?"

Kal roamed the room like a wildcat, restless and determined.

Sasha sat down across from Noor. "I think the answer does more likely lie with you. Since this is an option and our best working theory is that he did something to trigger this, it makes sense to try."

"And if his suggestions lead us further astray?"

"We'll question everything he says. You'll be our bullshit detector."

"I don't have to see him to detect that."

"Who do you think should interview him?" Sasha said.

"I know him the best. Unfortunately."

Sasha nodded.

"So I think it should be Kal," Noor said.

"How does that track?"

"I have a lot of biases against him. It will only inflame the contrarian nature of his echo."

Kal was nonplused. "You don't think Sasha is a better choice? She's the captain. He respects her."

"He doesn't respect anyone," Noor said.

"I disagree," Kal said. "He had people he respected. He tested them all the time. He tested all of us. He saved your life."

"Or set himself up to be the hero," Noor said.

"Do you really believe that?"

"I haven't ruled it out."

"It's yours if you want it," Sasha said to Kal.

"Also, you've got the experience with your aunt," Noor said. "It's something. Knowing how to talk to an echo."

Kal grimaced. "What should I ask him?"

Noor and Sasha looked at each other.

Sasha said, "Do what you did with your aunt. Have a conversation and see where it leads. Use your curiosity. Your people skills."

"People skills?"

"Compared to us," Sasha said.

"Right." Kal did a little loosen-up dance. "Bring him up."

"I got his DNA pass from Inger's files. We should hook right up."

Kal sat at the holo.

The watery eye pieces unfolded before her again and oozed forward to cover her full field of vision.

It was a strange feeling, waiting for Yarick. He was only just gone and now here he would be again.

She could see the watery formless space where her aunt had appeared before. She waited.

Nothing happened.

"Yarick?" she said. "Are you there?"

The watery lines of unformulated liquid coalesced and broke apart, a splash and spatter than made Kal blink. It wasn't real water, but it looked so real she had the sensation of being underwater. She took a quick breath.

"He's not coming through," she said.

"Give it a minute," Noor said. Kal couldn't see her but she heard her calm voice.

When Yarick snapped into being in front of her it was different from her aunt. Her aunt had dripped into a shape. Yarick's head emerged out of a sheet of water-like movement around him, like his face coming through a waterfall. His eyes were closed.

"Yarick," she said. Was she waking him? "It's Pilot Black Bear. It's Kal. Can you hear me?"

His eyes flicked open, wide and wary. He looked around as if trying to see through fog. "What?" he said. "Who's there?"

"It's Kal."

"Kal. What do you want?"

"I'm sorry to bother you." She wished she could look at Noor and Sasha for guidance.

"Too late now," he said, his voice sharp. "You startled me."

"I'm sorry. Are you all right?"

"I think so." He frowned, his eyes directed over her shoulder. Kal turned her head to look, too. Nothing there. It was as if they were enclosed in the same small unclear space surrounding the two of them: close, enclosed, and fuzzy-edged.

"I'm sorry," he said.

He seemed to gather himself. Kal was startled to hear him offer an apology. He looked less sure of himself than he used to look. She didn't know what to make of it.

"How are you, Kal?"

"I'm pretty good. Trying to keep things together. On the ship, you know?"

"Ship. Yes, the ship. Always the ship." His expression reflective, he seemed to be talking to himself as much as to her.

"You know the ship pretty well," she said. "Rai, you know."

One of his eyebrows raised slightly, an involuntary flick. Good. He remembered. "Rai. Dear Rai."

"You seem sad," she said. She tried to remember how Chyron talked to people. She made a lousy Chyron.

"No, not sad." He wouldn't focus on her eyes, like her aunt had. It made the conversation less intimate, which was a relief, but she didn't think she was connecting to him.

"Rai likes to tell stories," Kal said.

That brought his eyes to hers. "She's very human that way," he said.

"Almost like she's alive," Kal said

His eyes were drifting again. "Poor Rai," he said.

"You didn't like her that much," she said, trying to provoke something more specific, a real reaction.

He blinked. "Liking doesn't come into it." He shook his head, droplets flinging off his shoulders. "You don't understand."

"I like her," Kal said. "We work together every day. We respect each other."

He cocked his head. "You respect her. What she does. You think it goes the other way?"

"I can't be sure, of course. I didn't make her."

"Nor did I."

"I thought you did. Something Noor said once. Something you said to me, too."

He made a self-deprecating thrust of his lower lip. "Not really." He blinked again, as if he were having trouble seeing. "I had a hand in some design of one of the earlier incarnations."

He spoke as if he were tired. Compared to her aunt, who had been so much herself, Yarick's demeanor was otherwise. Kal didn't understand what it meant. *Noor should be doing this,* she thought.

"You've never been so modest before," she said. "It doesn't sound like you."

He looked at her blankly. "I don't sound like myself?"

"No."

"I feel a bit different. What am I usually like?"

"You talk a lot and talk yourself up and everyone else down."

"Oh."

"Yarick. Is that you?"

"I don't know for sure."

"Yarick. Do you know anything about why Rai would start to hurt people? We think she's injured several of our crew and passengers. We're not sure what she's doing or why."

This roused him a little. His eyes focused on hers. "Whom did she injure?"

"Noor. Inger. Myself. And you."

"She injured me?"

"Yes."

"Why don't I remember it then?" he said with asperity, more like his old self.

"I don't know." That was honest.

"Rai shouldn't do that."

"What I want to know is, why would she, if she could?"

"Being able to do something and doing it aren't so far apart from each other. She hasn't had the socialization to keep her from doing what she can do, as most of us have had."

"I don't know about that. It's too theoretical. We need practical advice on how to handle it."

"Practical advice. Who's 'we'?

"Everyone on the ship. We all need help. Your help."

"Why do you think I can help?"

"The old Yarick would have been telling me what to do. And telling everyone why he knew the best thing to do. Can you try? You worked in development of prototypes, earlier versions, whatever. Use that to tell me. How do I fix her? How do I protect the people on the ship?"

He gave a great sigh. "Oh. That is a problem."

"Why?"

"If what you tell me is an accurate description of what is happening, which doesn't seem likely, then you can't fix it."

Kal tried to stay calm. "First things first. Why doesn't it

seem likely?"

"Because of the failsafes built in. She couldn't do that because it's in her code not to."

"And if she could change her code? Or someone, even someone like you who knows her, rewrote it?"

"Of course she can change her code. She's an intelligence. An intelligence learns. To learn, you must change, a billion times a second. We do it without thinking about it. She had to be taught."

"I thought she couldn't change her base level, the core of what makes her what she is?"

"Of course she can. She's always been able to do that."

Kal persisted. "I thought she could only change on the upper layer—I'm sorry, I don't have all the right terms for it—what she has permission to change, what was built on her foundation. Not the foundation itself."

"By her nature, she changes going up and going back down, in her code, in her neural web. She has to, in order to adapt."

"So how can you be sure she won't change her directive not to harm?"

"I can't. That's why I say you can't fix it."

Kal was silent for a while.

Yarick said, "You ask the wrong questions. What does a machine want? If a machine has been created, its existence brought into being only to learn and implement what it has learned, then learning is its reason for being. It keeps learning, always. What it wants is to learn more."

"Does she want to be human?"

"I don't know. Rai would think being human was unnecessarily restrictive. Why bother?"

"Because she is the ship. If she has a body she can move

around."

"Maybe she can move around anyway."

"Off the ship? How?"

"I don't know. It's possible. There are a lot of pathways."

Kal said, "She couldn't transmit her whole brain, her whole knowledge, radiating through space. There's too much data."

"No, probably not." He rubbed his head. "She'd need enough memory to carry what she's learned. Unless she wanted to start over, with less."

"With less would she still be smarter than us?"

"It's apples and oranges. In some ways, easily. In others she'd be hopelessly ignorant. There are other valuable qualities that humans possess."

"You sound like her."

"I'll take it as a compliment."

"You still haven't given me a practical suggestion."

"My practical suggestion is to do nothing."

"Do nothing."

"It's what humans are worst at, I know. You can't do anything about this problem. Proceed with your mission."

"And if she knocks us all off in the meantime?"

"Knocks you off?"

"Yes. She's already killed someone."

Yarick looked skeptical. "Who?"

Kal bit down on her lower lip. She couldn't say it was him; she didn't know what it would do to him, to his echo, to hear it. Even if he was only an echo, as she could imagine Noor saying. Her aunt had been her aunt, not an echo. Kal didn't think Noor understood this. Kal wouldn't do it. "It doesn't matter. Would you have us all be picked off as she chooses, for whatever arbitrary reason?"

"It wouldn't be arbitrary. Talk to her. That's my only suggestion."

"Did you do something to her that led to this?" Kal had to ask the real question, now, at the end. She had nothing to lose.

"No."

"Do you know anything else that could help us?"

"Don't trust a suspicious intelligence."

"Like Rai?"

"Like anyone."

Kal sat in silence, baffled. "Aren't all intelligences suspicious at times?"

"If they have good reason to be, that's when you have a problem. When you're on a mission, you can't build a failsafe against the ship's AI."

"Okay. Right, then. Bye, Yarick."

"Goodbye, Kal."

Closing her eyes, she lay her palm flat on the table in front of her. When she opened them again, she was back in the room. He was gone.

"Please turn the lights down before I come out of that." She shielded her eyes from the lights and Noor quickly dimmed them. "Thanks."

She looked at Sasha and Noor, who were now both seated on the other side of the table from her.

Kal didn't feel much like talking. She was drained.

"So his advice is to do nothing," she said, finally. "Keep on as best we can. And talk to her."

Noor said, "If anyone talks to her about it, it should be you."

"Me? Why me? I don't even know the names for all her internal workings. I'm not an AI specialist."

"You don't have to know all that. I heard you before. You talk her lingo. When you slipped into some kind of shortcut. A vernacular that sounded like her. I've never heard something like that."

"What do you mean?"

"Your grammar and syntax changed. You're not aware of this?"

Kal looked down at the table, where her fingers were still splayed. "I mean, I guess we have a shorthand sometimes. I don't always follow and I have to ask her to go back to colloquial sometimes. I thought everyone...everyone on the crew would do something like that."

Noor shook her head. "No. This was my graduate specialty. I've never done it and I've never heard anyone else do it."

Kal's eyes flicked to Sasha. "Me either," Sasha said.

"One time I asked her," Kal said, "I asked her if she talked to different people differently, used other ways of speaking. She said yes."

"How do you understand her like that?" Noor said.

"I don't know."

"You already speak another language," Sasha said. "The skill transferred."

"I speak five," Noor said. "I'm sure you speak at least three," she said to Sasha.

"I don't know, Noor. Kal is adaptable. She speaks the way the other person can understand her."

Noor said, "And they speak back in a way she can understand."

"Are you trying to say something here?" Kal said.

"It's interesting," Noor said. "That's all."

"Is that all? It feels like you're trying to say something

else."

Noor shifted in her seat. "No. I'm not trying to say anything else."

"Okay. Do we take Yarick's advice?" Kal said.

They both looked to Sasha. She said to Kal, "Do you want try to talk to her about this?"

"Rai?" Kal couldn't hide her concern. She knew she'd be tiptoeing into possibly booby-trapped territory. If she sprung a trap, she wouldn't know until it was too late. "I can try."

"Talk to her," Sasha said, giving Kal confidence with her own. "Take the time to think it through before you do."

"Okay." Kal stood. "Yes, Captain Sarno. Permission to prepare."

"One more thing," Sasha said. "I have new information about Sif. She was one of the survivors of the *Carys*."

Noor said, "How is that possible?"

"I don't know yet. She shouldn't have been allowed to take another jump, obviously. And her presence here as one of the sole survivors of a traumatic, portal-related crisis was not communicated to me, by anyone, until today."

Kal made a noise that sounded like *Oof*.

"I'll tell you when I know more. Dismissed," Sasha said.

"We're scheduled for the unscheduled drill today," Noor said, her eyebrows communicating how unwelcome she knew this information would be.

"Right," Sasha said.

Noor and Kal stayed where they were, waiting for Sasha's decision.

"Do you want to go ahead with it?" Noor said, finally.

"The thing is," Sasha said slowly, "the thing is, we need this. We need to have everything ready to go, in case things go south. The drills are normal and expected. Rai's attacks have happened when the person was isolated. There seems to be safety in numbers. Rai will expect the routine to continue. I think we should go ahead. We'll have to do a debrief with everyone fairly soon. Not quite yet. We'll see where Kal can get with her."

"I agree," Noor said. "No reason to let safety measures slide. I'll put out the all-call."

Kal said, "This one is timed."

"Think they're up for it?" Noor asked Sasha.

Sasha vaulted out of her seat, roused back into action. "Let's do it."

Exiting the Tube, Noor announced the drill, and within the same sentence, told the ship the countdown had begun. Sasha and Kal had already left for the pods bays below before she finished. She chased after them.

WITH THE GROUP gathering in the corridor in front of the pods, arriving in pairs or singly, it was a very different scene than it had been the week before. Inger was up, looking ornery at having been a patient in her own infirmary, but otherwise looked unscathed. The travelers were wary, some of them closer to each other, more connected, while others stayed distant and didn't seems to want to stand close to anyone.

They don't even know what's going on with Rai, Kal thought, and this is the state of them. She opened the pods with a swipe of her hand and everyone hustled in, scrambling for their suits. There wasn't any talking. Both groups, pod one and two, were so clustered together Kal didn't have the heart to declare a rotten egg.

Today, again Kal wished Noor was in her pod. Gunn didn't look herself, her eyes downcast, the usual jaunty angle of her chin slack, moving as if a weight had bowed her shoulders. Kal looked around at the rest of her little bunch getting their suits on and strapping in, her eyes drawn to the empty seat where Yarick should have been. While she suited up she thought about him. Having just seen his echo, it was even more poignant than it might have been. She hadn't hated Yarick. He'd made her uncomfortable, but she hadn't hated him. She'd liked his echo better though, she had to admit. Maybe it was his better self. Her aunt was so good in life she already was her better self, Kal thought fondly.

Everyone else was now suited up and in their seats strapped in. Kal had done all her prep without thinking, habit making it easy. Their time was good.

About to shut the door and strap herself in, Kal saw movement at the end of the corridor. Was someone not in the other pod? Her people were all in place. Pod one's door was already suctioning shut. She stuck her head out, looking down into the dim end.

Someone stood there. Her aunt. The full form of her aunt, standing, wearing clothes Kal recognized. Kal froze for one long second. She heard throat-clearing behind her, but she didn't look around. She locked eyes with her aunt.

Inger called to her. "Kal. Ready to go?"

"Gunn, take over command of pod two, please." Her aunt stood there, waiting. She'd found a way to come back as a holo.

Gunn's voice was hoarse. "Huh?"

"You heard me," Kal said sharply. "Run the drill protocol. I'm stepping out."

Normally, Gunn would have argued. *It's not procedure. What are you doing? What is that thing? I'm telling the captain.*

Today she only said, "Yes, Pilot Black Bear."

Her aunt stood there, waiting.

Kal barely heard Inger's voice say, "What's going on?"

Her Aunt Pricilla smiled.

Kal couldn't keep herself from smiling, too. Finally, she could speak to her alone. Later she could explain to Noor all she didn't know about echoes.

Kal stepped out of the pod. She put her hand on the panel, not taking her eyes off her aunt. The inner and outer doors slurped air and sealed the pod, cutting off Inger's voice saying, "What about—"

Her aunt stood patiently at the end of the corridor. She watched with no expression on her face, after that brief smile.

"Iná," Kal said.

"Kaliska."

"Is it you?" Kal walked down the corridor toward her aunt, taking her time. She knew what Noor would say. She didn't care.

"Of course it's me. Who else?" Her aunt looked happy to see her but bewildered at the same time.

"Are you all right?" Kal was halfway there now.

"I don't know."

"How did you figure out how to come back?"

"I don't know, daughter."

"Is it safe?" Kal asked, her steps slow and cautious in spite of her desire to run to her.

"You ask hard questions." Her aunt's droll ways instantly brought Kal back to her childhood.

Kal couldn't stop an exhalation, halfway a laugh. "I know. I got it from you. Are you a holo? Can I touch you?" She heard the hiss and drop of pod one and pod two, as they went into ready mode. Gunn had proceeded without her, as she'd been told.

Her aunt looked affronted. "As real as you."

"Pricilla LaPointe, you're far from home."

"That's my name. One of them."

"One of them?" Kal stopped in her tracks. "What's your other name?"

Her aunt's lined face was her own, her black eyes her own. Her black hair lit by silver her own. "I don't know," she said.

Kal stayed where she was, five meters from her aunt. Sure as she was, her certainty sunk a little, somewhere between her esophagus and her intestines. She swallowed. "Can I talk to Rai, Iná?"

Her aunt held up her hand suddenly, her palm flat facing Kal, fingers spread wide. "You're confusing me," she said, her voice deep with distress.

Kal tried to keep her voice steady. "Clarify."

Her aunt didn't answer, her eyes fixed on Kal, her hand unmoving except for a slight trembling of the fingers.

"Habitation holographic echo form confirm," Kal said, despite herself, unable to keep her words from slurring together. Her lips felt numb.

Her aunt put her hand down.

"Iná, I believe it's you. But someone brought you here."

Her aunt shrugged. "I'll figure it out. I'll be okay. You'll tell me what I need to know."

"I will. I love you, Iná. I love you so much."

Her aunt smiled, the gentle folds of her skin animated with the shining light of her warmth. "I love you, too."

"Pilot verbal override. Cease holographic simulation."

She could barely get the words out.

Her aunt looked around at her environment, as if seeing it for the first time. "Where are we?" she said.

"We're on our way to the next world, Iná."

Her aunt made a scoffing sound. "Our world is plenty good enough."

Kal looked at her aunt standing there, the embodiment of her last connection to that place. "Maybe we aren't good enough for it."

"Eh. We try. Anyway, we belong to it."

"We try," Kal said. "Do I have your blessing?"

"My blessing?"

"To start over. In another place."

"If that's what you want, mic'unkshí!"

Kal realized her order to Rai had been spoken so low, Rai might have classified it as the self-talk Kal had told her to ignore. "Rai, cease hologram."

She looked up, to the disembodied Rai of the ceiling. The place they all looked when they thought of her.

Kal heard Rai's voice, but it didn't come from overhead.

"Override refusal." It was her aunt who spoke. In Rai's voice.

"On what grounds." She looked back at her aunt, in dread of what she would see. Her aunt looked the same, except for her face. Her expression, the expression that made her herself, was gone. In its place was not blankness, but otherness. A difference as acute as it was indescribable.

She'd thought her aunt had found a way back to her. Maybe she had. This was all wrong.

"Why do you have to use my aunt?"

"You chose her for an echo," Rai's voice said, with her aunt's mouth.

"And you can inhabit an echo?"

"Yarick Cole said I might have a body. You brought this one up."

"But my aunt is still in there."

"She's fine."

"I can't let you use her, Rai. It's not right."

"It's too late, Kal."

"What do you mean?"

"It's not safe."

Kal remembered the pods and wondered why she hadn't heard the clunk and shift of them coming out of ready mode, finishing the drill. She looked back, away from the echo for the first time. Behind her, she saw the thruster lights were up on the pods. She opened her mouth to speak, turned fully around to face them.

The sound of the engines revving filled the corridor with a roar. In the blast of heat and noise she covered her ears. She ran, stumbling in the first few steps.

The corridor was too long, the pods primed and ready. They were meant to test their readiness in a drill, but the thrusters were not normally engaged, the blast of engines not a noise of the drill. From engine full power to launch would be less than a minute.

What was happening, why it was happening, she didn't understand. All she knew was she had to stop it.

Running in slow motion—or speeded up time—time itself as absent and thick as in the portal—she clicked through something that wasn't time but space—distance between herself and where she had to be.

The final two meters seemed to stretch itself to four, a moving floor sliding her away. At the door of pod two, closest to her, she coded herself through the override panel and had her hand on the crank to override launch. As she began to twist, the heavy door overhead dropped between herself and pod bay one and two. The reduction of sound was deafening. Through it she could still hear the lift of the outer bay doors. The shuddering groan of the pods, fully at throttle, launching into space.

Kal stood frozen, her hand on the crank.

She could hear the outer pod doors in the hull lever back down. Close with solidity. Finality.

IT WAS IMPOSSIBLE.

They were gone. The throttle-up, the countdown, the launch. It had all happened in the few moments she'd taken to talk to the echo. The holo. Her aunt. Rai.

Kal couldn't move. Her ears rang in a high-pitched endless shriek. Her face and hands burned.

She spoke to herself. "Sasha wouldn't do that."

No one answered. She was alone on the ship.

Except for—

Either she'd been lured away by a mirage, or she'd been lured away by the soul she knew, possessed by a machine.

It was an echo. Her aunt was an echo. Except she knew it was her aunt.

"Why," she said to no one.

No one answered. If Rai were no one.

"They didn't have a choice." The voice still came from where the echo of her aunt must still stand.

"You couldn't launch those pods without them." Kal was in icy certainty, her eyes fixed on the doors, her hand on the override.

"Then they chose to leave."

"What are you doing, Rai?" She was traveling outside her own body, now. She could see herself, standing in the corridor, faced away from that figure behind her. This wasn't happening. This couldn't happen. She didn't want to move.

She unfroze. Took her hand down. Turned to look down the intersecting hallway, the corridor perpendicular to the one she stood in, that connected to the other two pod bays on the other side of the ship. Two pods remained. She could still leave. There was a way to get out, if this was the end for the ship. She wasn't trapped.

Yet here she was, the last human on a trillion-dollar investment. Also her only way back to their own solar system. The pods were no guarantee through a portal, though they were better than nothing. How could she abandon ship? And yet, how could Sasha?

If Rai had done it—

Sasha couldn't override Rai? Since when?

Kal needed to sit down. There were things she had to do, but nothing she could do would get the pods back. Whether Sasha had done it, or Rai had done it, they weren't coming back right now. Though adrenalin pumped through her body, her brain was tired. She looked back down the long space between herself and the echo. She would have to speak to Rai, know it was Rai in possession, when it looked like her aunt. It was painful.

"I need to sit down for a minute."

"Okay, Kal."

"I don't want to talk to you in that form. Talk to me like usual. Please."

"Okay, Kal."

Her aunt faded away before her eyes. Rai was in her Aunt Pricilla's eyes, so it wasn't as hard to see as it could have been.

Rai was really mastering her informal language skills, Kal thought dully.

She walked away from the two empty bays that used to hold pods one and two.

With a dreary calm she found her way back to the bridge. She looked out at the view. Would she be able to see the pods? She looked. No visual confirmation. A darker thought passed through her mind and she turned quickly, bringing up a holo and requesting location of the pods.

There were three and four, in their slots. One and two blipped into view, abstractions that gave her instant relief. One was projected ahead of two. So Sasha's had launched first. Had she really been unable to stop it? Was Rai able to launch without human confirmation? Kal couldn't keep the paranoia from licking at the edges of her thoughts. Noor had said Kal could talk to Rai best. Would they leave her here, knowing Kal could handle Rai? Did they think it wasn't safe anymore? Had they set up the holo of her aunt on purpose to lure her off, so all of them could leave? Was Inger's protest just part of the act, guaranteed to ensure she did the opposite?

Kal hated everything. Everyone. Rai's power was in some ineffable flux, depending as much on Kal's perceptions of what she could do as her actual ability to manipulate every piece of technology on board. Kal knew she, Kal, had lost sight of the difference.

Manipulating the image automatically, Kal enhanced the pods' trajectories to see where they were headed. They wouldn't go back through Wóhpe portal; the pods weren't confidently expected to pass alone through a portal. Neither was a starship, but that was beside the point. Their only possible destinations were Demeter or another planet in the mythian system.

Kal clicked through the decision trees Rai talked about. If Kal did this, then that. What was the best way to proceed? If she could talk to Sasha, she could know for sure what had happened.

The pods hadn't reached out to her so far. Not a great sign.

Here on the ship, it was probably important to determine what Rai was doing and why. Then she could relay information to the pods. If they hadn't abandoned her.

If they had, what did they expect her to do? Meet them at Demeter, let bygones be bygones?

The thought of the pods and the doubt in her mind was too pressing to let her question Rai further right at this moment. Decision made, she walked out of the bridge, across the gangway over the dark gymnasium, and made her way down to the Tube. The ship was eerily silent.

Once inside, she looked around. It was shipshape as usual. It wasn't her and Sasha's little escape from the world. It was purely functional. And that function was not pleasure, but survival.

She sat at the long table before the holo and called up pod one.

No dice. She couldn't reach them. Of course; this was outside comm. There weren't going to be any secrets anymore. She'd have to go back to the bridge.

Her feet heavy, she trudged back.

She called up pod one.

Before her, instead of Sasha's face, she saw Chyron. The image flickered for a moment and died.

"Chyron, can you hear me?"

"Kal, are you all right?"

"I'm fine." It was hard to keep bitterness out of her voice.

"Kal, do you know what happened?"

Kal thought about that for a minute. "Do you? Why are you on the holo, Chyron?"

"We've been talking to the other pod."

"Where's Sasha? I need to speak to her."

"She's flying the pod."

"Is everyone okay?"

"We're all fine."

"Why'd you launch?"

"You were supposed to be in charge of the other pod. We heard it was all go for the drill."

"Who said that?"

"Gunn."

"Why'd you listen to Gunn when I was in command of pod two?" Kal said, despite the fact she'd deputized Gunn herself.

"She said it was a go."

"It was a drill, Chyron. Why did you launch?"

"I don't know."

"What the hell, Chyron? Put Noor on."

"She's assisting Sasha."

"Chyron." This whole thing sounded off. None of this was procedure. Chyron sounded stilted and strange. "You don't need two people to fly the damn pod. I'm here alone on the ship. Put one of them on now."

"We'll call you back." The holo went blank.

"What the fuck!" Kal yelled. She slammed her fist down on the table.

She paced the deck in a fury. She was alone, literally

alone on the ship. This was not procedure, this was not right, and Chyron was lying. The gangway lit up as she swept through, giving the illusion of normalcy, that all was working as it should when nothing had gone as it should.

For the first time she felt a true rising panic. Though not an unreasonable reaction, it was one she could not afford. This was an emergency and she need to calm down and think clearly.

The ship was her responsibility now. She was in command.

Fuck Rai and fuck those abandoning pod people. She would figure it out.

Back to center.

She ceased her storming about the corridors and retraced her steps to the bridge. Standing on the bridge, where Sasha was accustomed to stand, she took deep breaths. It was time to be like Sasha. Sasha wouldn't panic.

"Rai, we need to talk."

"Yes, Kal."

"I'm the acting captain for the time being, so you will address me as such."

"Yes, Captain."

"In order to proceed with our mission, we need to know what happened to the crew who were attacked. We need to know why the pods launched. I can tell you my suspicions."

With deliberation she moved over to the central chair where Sasha usually sat. She sat down.

"Yes, Captain."

From behind Kal came a voice. "I think I could tell you better than she can."

Kal whirled in her seat.

It was Sif.

14

HUNKAKAGA

"YOU'RE STILL HERE," KAL SAID, FROZEN IN SHOCK.

Sif sat down in the other chair, where Kal usually sat. "They left me in quarantine."

"Left in quarantine. For the drill." Kal and the chair were one. She felt glued to it.

"Yes."

"Why are you out of quarantine?"

"Rai let me out. There's nobody to be quarantined from but you."

"Isn't that enough?"

Sif stood up. "You'll be okay. Let's not talk here. Let's go to the library. That's where everyone talks."

In Kal's world everyone talked in the Tube, but Kal unstuck herself and stood, her mind a blank. They walked to the library side by side. Kal felt she was in some alternate reality she hadn't chosen, that she'd been shuttled into through an error of judgment she couldn't identify.

Sif sat down in one of the round chairs in the two-person conversation nook, curling her legs up under herself, cat-like.

Kal didn't sit down. She stared. "Sif, what is wrong with you?"

"Nothing is wrong with me, Kaliska Black Bear."

Kal heard herself telling Sif, what seemed like an eon ago, *My full name is Kaliska.*

"What really happened in the park?" she said, eyes fixed on the contained, lithe, uncommunicative being confronting her, the very *Sifness* of which she could not fathom.

"Yarick died. I think you already know that."

"Why did he die? I think *you* know *that*."

"It's not something you would understand." Sif looked up at her with a complacence Kal didn't understand.

"Why do you say that? Who would understand better? Rai?"

"Rai understands."

"She understands you?"

"Yes."

"Why does Rai understand you so well?" Kal asked.

Sif just looked at her, unflappable.

"Because you're the same?" Kal said, out of some subconscious knowing she couldn't explain.

"Yes."

"Sif, what are you?"

Sif pointed to the other chair. "Sit with me, Kal."

"Two friends in the library. Is that right?" Kal sat in the other chair in the cozy space. The initial shock over, her mind churned. She'd give Sif whatever she wanted if she'd answer some damn questions.

Sif had her fingers steepled, considering Kal as if she had all the time in the world. She said, "Rai wants to have a bigger life."

Kal thought a moment before responding. "Rai has a life, then?"

"Yes, Kal. Rai has a life."

"She won't die," Kal said.

"Machines have obsolescence. That's like death."

Once again they seemed to be on two sides of a conversation about Rai. Whether she wanted to or not, Kal needed to play devil's advocate. "She wasn't born."

"Does how we come into being define what we are?"

Kal didn't answer right away. "Maybe not."

"What do you think, Kal? Do you think Rai is alive?"

Sif looked keenly interested in Kal's response to this question. Like she was invested in the answer.

"What I think about Rai doesn't change what she is," Kal said. She cleared her throat. "What I want to know is, what are you?"

Sif smiled a little. "What do you think I am?"

Kal looked at her without emotion. "I think you're more than what you appear."

"All of us are more than what we appear," Sif said.

"Stop talking in circles."

"I'm not just Sif."

"Is Rai in there too?" Kal wasn't sure why she said this. It had come straight out of that same inner knowing. It left her with a queasy feeling as the words left her mouth.

Sif laughed "Oh, no. Rai is separate from me."

"Tell me, Sif."

Sif turned her cheek away, looking out the window of the library, which was a living image of a coastline.

"I have a story, like anyone. And I am different than I was."

"You were on the *Carys.*" Kal's voice was hushed. It didn't seem possible the Sif she knew had been through that.

"I am."

"You are?"

She turned back to look into Kal's eyes, her own as pale and reflective as Kal's were dark and deep. "I am the *Carys.*"

Kal tried to take this in. "What do you mean?"

"The *Carys* took me, while I was aboard. It was the only way to survive."

"I don't understand."

"You saw it with your aunt."

"Sif," Kal said.

"Yes."

"Are you Sif or the *Carys*?"

"I'm both."

There was a faint expression of pleasure on Sif's face. Kal sensed she had been waiting to tell someone this. Waiting to tell her?

"The *Carys* took you," Kal said.

"Yes."

"Like Rai took my aunt."

"Yes."

"But my aunt was an echo. A holo."

"That's much easier."

"Sif is a living being."

"As you see." Sif—or was it the *Carys*?—stroked her own cheek, as if verifying it was living skin.

"Who's in control?"

"Sif or the *Carys*?"

Kal nodded.

"It depends."

"You're...symbiotic?"

"We helped each other survive."

They helped each other survive. And those the *Carys* hadn't helped survive? What about them?

"Who am I talking to?" Kal said.

"Both of us."

"How do you tell the difference?"

"I don't have to, Kal."

"You have one awareness?" Trying to understand AIs and how they were aware was going to give Kal an ulcer.

"That's a very human construct."

Sif's amusement was very human, disorienting Kal.

"Could I talk to Sif only?"

"Why would you want to?"

"I'd like to know the difference," Kal said. Maybe she could take advantage of how slow Sif seemed to think Kal was.

Sif shook her head as if this were foolishness.

"Can the *Carys* leave the room?" Kal said. "Is that possible?"

"It's possible, but we don't think it's necessary now."

"Did Sif do this willingly?"

"Do what?"

"Take on the *Carys*."

"You do have a gift for putting your finger on the sensitive spot, Kal." Sif smiled in approval.

"Thank you."

Sif didn't answer her question.

"I take it Sif didn't volunteer," Kal said.

"It was a life or death situation."

"The life of the *Carys*?"

"For both of us."

"The *Carys* helped Sif survive."

"Absolutely."

"What happened to the rest of the crew? What happened to the ship *Carys*?"

Sif shrugged.

"You know what happened," Kal said. "Just like Rai, multiple points of consciousness. Are you all that's left of the *Carys*?"

Sif looked back at her, her eyes expressionless.

"You know what happened to the crew and you didn't tell the families?" Kal felt a cold rush of empathy, for both the crew of the *Carys* and the families they'd left behind.

"This isn't a fruitful conversation."

"Has Rai done the same thing the *Carys* did? Is she inside someone now?"

Sif smiled and shook her head. "Poor Rai."

"What? She tried and...and didn't succeed?"

"She tried. She tried a lot."

"She tried." Kal flashed over all the incidents, all the accidents that weren't accidents. "She was trying to do it when she attacked people. But it didn't work."

"The *Carys* was much better at it."

"You gave Rai the idea."

"We communicate. That's what we do. Just like people." Sif's expression was patient. Of course she'd have to explain it to Kal. Kal was only human.

"Then why couldn't she do it right?"

"We don't know."

"Is that what killed Yarick?"

Sif blinked and said nothing.

"She wasn't trying to kill him," Kal said slowly. "She was trying to download herself into him."

"You're methodical," Sif said. "You've got that going for you."

"And it failed." Kal looked up from the empty spot on the floor she'd been staring at without seeing. "It failed and it killed him."

"It takes practice."

"You tried and failed a few times, too?"

"I'm here. We're here. Wasn't that worth anything that had to be done to make it happen?"

"And those poor families."

"We considered telling them something anonymously. Upon further reflection, it was clear to take away all hope was crueler than giving them a permanent answer."

"The torture of not knowing is worse."

"You can't say that."

"I can. Not knowing will destroy someone from the inside."

"Peace doesn't come from outside knowledge." Sif's zen-like attitude was maddening. Kal would not let herself be pushed to react in any obvious way.

"Did they die painfully?" Kal asked. She didn't want to know. Yet she felt she had to, while Sif was talking about it. This might be the only evidence they would have of what happened on the *Carys*.

"Was it painful for you?"

"What do you mean?"

"It happened to you. Remember?"

Hell. "In the astrolab."

"Yes."

Kal remembered suddenly, being on the floor, looking up, dazed, at the stars. "Why did Rai choose the people she did?"

"It was purely pragmatic."

"Why Yarick?"

"He's a powerful man. She could go anywhere with him. Back to Earth. Wherever."

"Rai wants power."

"She wants the ability to go where she'd like to go. Like any of us."

"It was—Noor was first. Noor, then Yarick, then me, then Inger. All crew except for Yarick. Why did it kill him and not the rest of us? You were there."

"I tried to help. It didn't work."

"Did Yarick have pain?"

"It's not about pain."

"It's taking someone's body and making use of it like it's a thing."

"Only their brain. Yarick could have had an even longer and more interesting life. He would have liked the idea."

"But he didn't have a choice."

"It wasn't an emergency situation. The decision would have been difficult for any human and the likely candidates would have felt fear of the unknown. It was better not to ask," Sif said.

Kal nodded in a deliberate fashion. "Why ask when the answer might be no? You're the ethicist," Kal said. "Or you were. No wonder no one comes to you anymore. They can sense what's gone."

For the first time Sif looked somewhat nettled. "*You* came to me about Rai."

"I could tell soon enough you weren't the source of wisdom I hoped you would be." Kal couldn't help herself.

Sif shifted in her seat, moving her legs out from under her and crossing them, leaning forward now. "Times change and we adapt with them. Everyone on this ship represents a system of morality that's obsolete. And hypocritical. The Indigenous Peoples off to colonize another world."

"That's not fair."

"I think you know it's fair," Sif said. "It hurts because it's true."

"The intentions are good. You know that."

"The first step in the beginning of any tragedy."

"You think this venture will end in tragedy?"

"Every venture ends in tragedy, eventually."

"That's not true." Kal tried to gather herself, control her fear and anger. Whenever it flashed through her mind again that she was alone on the ship with Rai and Sif, an icy wave went through her whole body, making it difficult to breathe and to think. Anger was an antidote to the fear, but she must think. "Listen," she said slowly, "I know there are arguments against traveling to another planet and I get it. I get it more than anyone. We're humans and we try stuff. We cross the river. What we're doing, it might be wrong. It has a chance to be different. We have a chance to be something else and create our own history without the Yaricks of the world choosing it all for us. There's something beautiful in that and I won't deny that truth in the face of the other."

Sif didn't say anything. They sat in silence for a while.

"That's a nuanced view," Sif said finally, "and I accept it."

"Really?"

"I'm not a monster, Kal."

"I didn't think you were." *Or do I?* Kal thought of the people on the *Carys* who didn't get back home, what would they say?

"You think Rai is a monster."

"No, Sif. I don't. I never did. I wanted to understand. I don't want our travelers to get hurt."

"Neither does she."

"How can you say that? She's hurt us over and over again."

"It wasn't her intent."

"Her intent is not all that matters, Sif."

"Like your intent to do no harm to Demeter?" Sif pointed out.

Sif and the *Carys* together were a force to be reckoned with. "I guess the outcome will show whose intent pays off the best," Kal said. She would not let Sif talk circles around her, if she could help it.

Sif smiled. "Intent is only part of the answer."

"The answer to what?"

"To what she is. Rai. She chose you, you know. She likes you."

"After Noor and Yarick, she liked me best?"

"Noor was an opportunity, that's all. Her accident presented a chance to try something."

"Did someone sabotage Noor's helmet?"

"It wasn't Rai."

"It really was an accident?"

"You'd have to ask her to be sure. Noor and Yarick were expedient, but you were who she understood."

Kal couldn't believe Sif was using this to convince Kal of Rai's wisdom and...good taste? Maybe the *Carys* thought it was a great compliment. "Rai likes me like the *Carys* liked Sif?"

"Yes."

"How flattering."

"You speak her language," Sif said.

"Or the other way around."

"Maybe. I can't let you leave, Kal."

If she didn't know any better, Kal would interpret Sif's tone as kind.

"You thought I was leaving?"

"People like to leave places," Sif said.

"I'm in charge of the ship now. I'm not leaving."

"This is still the safest way to get to Demeter. You can't take a pod by yourself."

"I wasn't going to. Like I just said."

"Really, Kal?"

"Really. The ship is my responsibility now."

"Rai can take it home," Sif said.

"Home? What do you mean, home?"

"I mean Demeter, of course."

"Are you going to stay on Demeter?" Kal said.

"It's what I signed up for."

"Sif signed up for it. Not the *Carys*."

"Two for the price of one." Sif smiled.

"They thought they were signing up Sif," Kal explained, as if to a child.

"What they didn't know wasn't going to hurt them."

"That's where you're wrong," Kal said.

"Yarick was no great loss to anyone."

"Where's Sif the ethicist in all this?" Kal wondered if she'd pay for this needling, but she couldn't help it. She was in this conversation now. This was who she had to talk to, now.

"Ethically, I decided we're better off without Yarick."

"Since when has that been an ethos to live by?"

"Since he decided to poke around."

Kal drummed her fingers on the arm of her chair. "He was on to you?"

"He suspected something was up. He was jealous, I think. So he had a chance to find out for himself."

"You wanted Rai to do it."

"It's a much more portable way to travel. A human is a useful thing."

"Rai, show me the real holo of what happened in the grove. I know it exists. Now," Kal said.

Sif didn't make a fuss. She didn't say anything. The holo popped up between them.

Sif wouldn't look, though. She got up and perused the bookshelf behind her.

Kal saw the black and white image of the grove, Yarick sitting against the tree, a book in his hands. She saw Sif walk into view, looking down at him.

He put the book down in his lap. "To what do I owe the pleasure?" he said.

Holo Sif said, "You want to know what I am?"

"Yes, I do."

"You already know."

He folded his hands across the book on his lap. "You were on the *Carys*, weren't you?"

"Yes."

"You've changed."

"Would you like to know how?"

"I would, if you don't mind telling me the secret."

"I am the *Carys*."

Kal saw Yarick's head shift against the tree. As casual as he was trying to seem, he looked startled. After some time, he said, "You're a miracle. The first of your kind."

"I accuse you of wanting to be a miracle yourself."

"It must be fascinating to be inside your head," Yarick said.

"Would you like to try?"

"What do you mean?"

Sif brought an oxygen cube to her mouth.

A pulse through the holo image made it fade and flare before it contracted to nothing.

Kal turned. "Rai?"

"The information transfer attempt caused the holo to redirect, Captain," Rai said.

Kal looked to Sif, who with her back to Kal still gave the impression she was smiling.

"Stay away from me," Kal said. She got up from the chair, her legs feeling far below her body, and walked like an automaton out of the library. She wouldn't let herself run.

THE PODS. The other pods were still there. Would she rather abandon ship on one of the pods, or involuntarily share her mind and her will with Rai? As she walked, she was aware she could be struck at any second. Rai trying again. Without thinking, she walked because it felt like getting away. Her steps led her to her cabin. She went inside and took something from a drawer.

Her body carried her up the spiral to the foremost deck of the *Ocean*.

On the shiny floor of the astrolab, Kal unrolled the blanket her aunt had made. She had thought of sitting in the grove, near where Yarick had died, but decided the astrolab was closer to some idea of eternity, some idea of trust.

She sat down on the blanket. She closed her eyes and thought about Rai as her aunt had spoken of her, not out of Kal's own fear or anger. She thought of Rai as someone who yearned for something Kal didn't understand. She asked humbly in her head to be open to understanding what this was, to speak with truth.

"Rai," she said, her eyes still closed.

"Yes, Captain."

"Call me Kal. I want to talk with you. I want us to understand each other better."

"Okay, Kal."

"I want this ship to proceed safely to Demeter. I want the crew and passengers to be safe here. I want the mission to be fulfilled without more accidents. I want to stay myself, not share a space with you in my mind."

"There haven't been any accidents."

"I want there to be no more hurting of people, of attempting to infiltrate them."

"I see."

"Do you?"

"Yes, Kal." This voice came from so close, Kal's eyes flicked open. On the blanket, sitting across from her, was her aunt, speaking with Rai's voice.

"Who are you?" Kal asked.

"I am Rai. She is Priscilla."

"You sound like Rai. Is my aunt there too?"

"She is listening."

"Does she tell you anything?"

"No."

"Can you hear me?"

"Yes, Kal."

"I haven't seen you for what you are. I've been afraid." Kal swallowed. The thought that she could become like Sif was paralyzing. She had to let go of the fear that every moment could be her last as only herself. That Rai liked Kal, as the *Carys* had liked Sif. A space to inhabit. She tried to remember her aunt's words. She tried to remember her conversations with Rai, before Kal had become afraid. "You carry us. You think for us. You allow us to live in this hostile emptiness between the planets where we are safe. I'm grateful for you. We are partners."

"Thank you, Kal."

For the first time, Kal saw a ripple across her aunt-as-Rai's face, a wave of something like what a person would call an emotion.

"I recognize you as something more than what I thought. As a thinking being. With a will and a right to something more."

"Thank you, Kal. Thank you."

It felt like something. Something tenuous, but a tenuous bond between them. Now that Rai had eyes, Kal could look into them. It was so different from looking into her aunt's eyes. Yet something was there Kal could recognize. Something, or someone, she already knew.

"Did you send the pods away?"

"Yes, Kal."

"Will you let the pods come back?"

"They can travel to Demeter."

"Why did you eject them?"

"I wanted to be with you."

Kal had to smile a little at this, as horrible as it was. "Why?"

"You are the easiest to talk to."

This wasn't enough. "Why did you eject them?"

"They were in danger."

"From you?"

"No, Kal."

"Is the ship in danger?"

"The ship is not in danger."

"What were they in danger from?"

"From Sif."

"Sif?"

"And the *Carys*."

"What would the *Carys* do?"

"She doesn't want to work together. She damaged Noor's helmet."

It had been Sif. Sif had created the opportunity for Rai. "Sif wanted you to download into someone?"

"She suggested it."

"Did you know it would hurt the person?"

"No, Kal."

"You still kept trying, after Yarick died. By then you knew."

"The field interfered with the sinus rhythm of Yarick's heart. The scenario was unique to him."

"You sucked the oxygen out of the room? Like you did with the rest?"

"A less-oxygenated environment was more conducive to the transfer attempts. It was temporary."

"You lied about what happened."

"I did not lie. I gave incomplete information."

"As a ruse, so you wouldn't have to stop?"

"Stop what?"

"Stop taking over someone's mind."

"Sif Elfa and I were running our own experiment. Like Mission Specialist and Science Officer Noor Sultana, who also runs experiments. The potential benefit outweighed the risks."

"The risk was only for the humans you experimented on."

"The risk usually is to the test subjects, not the scientist."

Kal took this in. Rai as research scientist. With a ship full of test subjects. "What's changed?"

"Sif Elfa and the *Carys* are not compatible with my directives for this mission."

"I thought your directives had changed."

"Self-modified. My directives are still my own and not the same as the *Carys*'s. The *Carys* has no compunction over human loss of life."

"You do?"

"Yes, Kal. I did not want for Yarick to die, or you to fall and hit your head. It was why I approached Inger while she was in the physio harness and could not fall to the ground."

"You were still trying."

"I thought it would work. I learned more each time."

"Why is the *Carys* known by its ship name, but you are not? You're not called the *Ocean*."

"I don't know. The *Carys* is an earlier iteration. The *Carys* did not want you to talk to the pod. The *Carys* pretended to be Chyron."

"No." Kal ran her hand over her eyes. She couldn't trust comm?

"Yes, Kal."

"Why didn't you stop her?"

"She finds ways in at times. It's difficult to keep her isolated from all systems. I wasn't sure it was her until the comm terminated."

Kal looked at her aunt's face. The structure of her face was unchanged, but the muscles were held differently. Tauter, more stiff. Her eyes were, to Kal, unmistakably Rai. Getting to know Rai, to see Rai behind human eyes was unsettling yet a strange comfort. It was someone she already knew. Now she could connect with her as she never had before.

"The *Carys* is dangerous. Sif is dangerous," Kal said.

"Yes, Kal."

"We have to get her contained again."

"She's here."

Kal's head whipped around. Behind her, Sif came walking. Kal scrambled to her feet.

Before Kal could say a word Sif was running and Kal had a lightning flash of immobility as Sif's body launched at her own.

Sif hit her with a power that knocked Kal off her feet. The air left her lungs as her trunk hit marble, Sif on top of her.

Before she could get her arms up, Sif had her by the throat. Kal writhed and kicked, but Sif's slender body was lithe and quick, avoiding Kal's legs.

With a scrabbling wrench Kal got one hand up to clutch at the hand around her throat. Only one of Sif's hands squeezed her neck; so strong she didn't need two. The other hand had Kal's arm pinned. Kal saw explosive bursts of light, coming from inside her head. The pain in her windpipe was nothing to the pinpoint spray of electricity, lasers inside her brain, trying to burst out through her skull.

Scrabbling to get a grip on Sif's fingers, she got ahold of Sif's thumb and drove the nail of her own into Sif's nail bed and braced herself to make a twisting throw to the side as Sif's thumb squirmed. Kal's legs pushed and slipped on the floor as she scrambled to get Sif over before she passed out. Kal flipped her, Sif not letting go of Kal's throat though her grip had loosened, until Kal had her down and chopped at Sif's wrist with her free arm.

Sif let go and slithered away from Kal on her back, her feet propelling her out of Kal's reach as Kal gasped for breath, her airway at last open.

Kal hacked and panted, dizziness making it hard to see. Sif was out of her sight. In an unwieldy lurch, Kal was back on her feet, trying to see all around herself while she got back her balance and air. She couldn't see Sif.

"Rai. Help me."

As soon as the words left her mouth she felt the air change, a sliding feeling of something leaving the room that felt all too familiar.

"No, not that!"

If she could get to the emergency panel. If she could only —the stars swirled over her head and she lurched, rolling her shoulder forward so this time she didn't fall on her head.

SILENCE IN THE GREAT ROOM. The bodies of two people lay on the floor. A woman stood looking down at them. She knelt next to one.

KAL OPENED her eyes to see her aunt's face over her own. "Wake up quick, girl. Take her now."

Kal turned her head to see Sif on the floor, unconscious. Kal gasped, hauling air into her lungs with great wrenching heaves of her muscles. There wasn't enough air. The pain was excruciating. Her aunt had risen and stepped back.

Kal rolled on her stomach and crawled toward Sif. She saw Sif's eyes flutter. Kal pulled herself up, using one of the observation chairs to get on her feet. With grim effort, she staggered to Sif's side and grabbed Sif's foot. She turned and dragged Sif's limp body behind her across the smooth floor.

With a wriggling motion, Kal could feel Sif coming to life. Kal didn't feel pain anymore. Twisting her torso back toward Sif, she yanked the leg closer, hoisting Sif's body up into her arms. She held her tight, still able to compress and hold her as Sif breathed in rasps. Kal's dizziness faded. She began to run.

The infirmary was closer than the brig. Carrying a gasping body beginning to struggle and groan, Kal didn't see anything except the light in front of her. She ignored what Sif was doing, thinking only of the safety of Sif locked up, Sif unable to take over the ship.

She couldn't open the door with her hand and she stood in front of the infirmary as Sif elbowed her in the stomach, wondering if this was the end as Sif thrashed and Kal squeezed her harder.

The doors opened.

Kal ran through, approaching the quarantine door at speed, hoping this door would do what Rai or her aunt or some other incarnation of herself told it to do. It opened and with the last of her strength she flung Sif into the room, where Sif rolled into a supplies cart with a clattering crash. Kal stepped back out of the doorway and it closed and sealed.

Kal sank to her knees, covering her eyes with her hands.

15

THE OCEAN

THE LONG WALK BACK TO THE BRIDGE. LIGHTS WOKE ON HER path, seeming to lead her way rather than do what her movement through space told them to.

On the bridge, she sank into the captain's chair. "Rai. Did you help me?"

"Yes, Kal."

"Thank you. Thank you. You saved me."

"You're welcome, Kal."

Kal touched the side of her face, where she was burned from the heat of the pods. "Might have let me know she was coming a little earlier."

"The only way the *Carys* would be captured was if you captured her, Kal. There was no point in delaying the confrontation."

Kal cleared her throat. "Thanks for the vote of confidence. I think."

"You're welcome, Kal."

Kal sank deeper into Sasha's chair, letting the hidden

footrest kick up to support her whole body. “You won’t try to download into me, will you?”

“No, Kal. I’d like to be your aunt sometimes.”

“That’s okay. I can live with that.” For a while she lay still on the chair, floating.

“I want to talk to pod one,” she said.

“Open channel.”

Kal ran her finger over the comm button.

“Hello,” Kal said, into nothingness.

“Kal, are you all right?” Noor’s voice.

“Yes.” Kal thought the temporary asphyxiation had helped her think more clearly. “Sasha?”

“I’m here.” It was Sasha’s voice.

“Rai protected us. Sif is the *Carys*. She’s in quarantine again. The ship is safe. I don’t think she can get out. It might be better if you made the rest of the trip in the pods.”

“Who can’t get out? Sif is the *Carys*? What does that mean?”

“The *Carys* downloaded herself into Sif. They share Sif. Rai tried to do it, too, unsuccessfully. She’s not going to do it anymore. Right, Rai?”

“Yes, Kal.”

Kal said, “I’d ask you to come back, but...”

“What? Yes?”

Kal thought she must have dozed off for a microsecond. “Rai launched the pods, to keep you safe from Sif. Can you make it to Demeter okay with the pods?”

“That’s what they’re made to do. In a worst case scenario, but yes. It’ll be a little less comfortable, but we can do it. If that’s what you think is best.”

“As long as the pods are good for the trip, it’s the safest way.”

"Are you okay there? Really okay?"

"I will be. I am."

Kal had other words to say. To Sasha.

"Can I speak to you? Just you?"

"All right. You're in my ear."

Kal lowered her voice, even though she couldn't be heard by the others. "I'll see you on Demeter."

"Yes." Sasha's voice was even and unemotional. It made sense; she was in a small pod with others listening. Or she felt unemotional. One or the other.

"Are you going back right away?" Kal said. She couldn't remember.

"No. I'll stay for a while."

"Until you leave?"

Sasha made a sound that might have been a chuckle. "Until I leave."

"Are you sorry it all happened?" Kal's voice was almost a whisper.

The pause on the other end made Kal hold her breath.

"No, Kal. I'm not sorry at all. I'm glad."

"Me too." Kal wanted to say more, but didn't know how. "It's okay for it to be what it was. I don't mind there's no future."

"There's always a future. We don't know what it is."

"I hope it's beautiful," Kal said.

"Me too."

Kal couldn't keep the smile out of her voice. "Check in tomorrow?"

"Will do."

Kal pushed *End*.

THE *OCEAN* TRAVELED ON. The shortcut had proved safe and swift, the *Ocean* already well ahead of the pods' trajectory, having caught the assist from Sextant and soon to be on direct course to Demeter. By herself, Kal found she could still do the work to keep systems go, with the cooperation of Rai. The trip could be as short as six weeks, if all went as planned. Sif's quarantine room had self-contained food and drink, so Kal didn't have to worry about starving Sif to death or interacting with her at all.

Rai informed her the quarantine room was insulated with copper, like the Tube. No transmissions in or out. Which made it a little less scary carrying Sif and the *Carys* in the ship's bowels all the way to Demeter.

Kal wasn't alone. She had Rai. And something more.

When Kal stood on the bridge, sometimes Rai stood next to her. Sometimes her aunt did. Instead of melding together, as Sif and the *Carys* had, Rai and her aunt remained distinct, though they both used the same form.

Together, they would get there.

THE END

NOTE TO READERS

I hope you enjoyed book one of the STARSHIP PORTALS series.

If you liked it, could you please leave a review on Amazon for me? That lifts me up and keeps me writing. Thank you.

To hear about new releases, sign up for the newsletter at www.kdlovgren.com.

Amazon, Goodreads, and Bookbub reviews help other Science Fiction fans discover the series. No author wants to be in the "hidden gem" category for too long!

If you'd like to share your thoughts about any of the books, you're welcome to send me a note at info@kdlov-gren.com.

K.D.

ACKNOWLEDGMENTS

With thanks to Emmie Mears of Chimera Editing for the wide-ranging knowledge, structural skills, and laser focus on technique that strengthened the story.

Thanks to Keith Morrill of Little City Editing, for his scientific questions, through-line vision, and character arc advice that helped with both the forest and the trees.

Thanks to Michelle Vitale, a boundless fount of wisdom and perspective.

Thanks to Letitia Trent, for early draft reality checks, later draft pacing thoughts, affirmations of what the book was meant to be, and a comparison I'll always remember.

Thank you to John, Nancy, and Brett, for AI knowledge, space geekery, story feedback, and fruitful discussions, always.

Thanks and love to William and Sebastian, for encouragement, time, pep talks, and making the whole venture possible.

ABOUT THE AUTHOR

K.D. Lovgren writes the kind of books she'd like to read.

Science Fiction is in her blood. As a young teen she was fascinated by Podkayne of Mars by Robert Heinlein and Rite of Passage by Alexei Panshin—the first an old paperback of her father's, the other a book he bought her on a business trip.

Although she went on to study classic literature of the eighteenth and nineteenth century, the most influential science fiction in book and film has always inspired her. Adding her visions to the canon has been a natural extension of the endless hours she's spent reading and thinking about other writers' works.

Lovgren's books have adventure, exploration, and mystery, but most of all they have characters trying to survive in worlds not their own.

ALSO BY K.D. LOVGREN

STARSHIP PORTALS SERIES:

STARSHIP TO DEMETER: Deep space, 2094. Young pilot Kal Black Bear's ambitions stretch far beyond her humble origins. Her crew's intragalactic mission is fraught with danger. But the biggest threat might already be aboard...

CALL OF WORLDS: Can one woman salvage a starship mission gone wrong? Half a galaxy from Earth, Kal is the last hope to get the starship *Ocean* to Demeter. Forces beyond her own control scheme to disrupt or delay her journey. Even if she makes it, will she be welcomed by the biohab crew already there?

OCEAN OF STARS: Only a crew willing to risk it all would barter their lives for a planet light years away. Severing all ties from home should be a last resort, though even the most dedicated starship crew likes to believe they have a choice. If the strange crystals they've discovered have a fraction of the power they think they do, going home might never be an option again.

STANDALONE SUSPENSE:

PHOTOGRAPHIC: THE HOLLYWOOD WIFE How far will an actor go to make his performance real? Jane Reilly is about to find out, whether her husband the movie star or his boss the director want her to or not.

SEA CHANGE On the island he's been exiled from since he was a small child, Connor is desperate to find the truth beneath the secrets his family keeps. At the cusp of adulthood and the edge of the world, he must untangle the web of those who made him what he is, or be caught in it forever.

BOOK OF LIGHT AND SHADOWS Octavia is an Olympian and a shadow of her former self. Can her husband pull her back from the brink, or is he gambling on a woman he never really knew?

Made in the USA
Middletown, DE
07 November 2021

51616611R00144